FOREST BOOKS

THICKHEAD
AND OTHER STORIES

HALDUN TANER (1916–1986) was born in Istanbul, the son of
Ahmet Selâhattin, a lawyer who represented Istanbul in the last
Ottoman Chamber of Deputies. In 1935, after completing his
primary and secondary education at Galatasaray, he went to
study economics and political science at Heidelberg, returning
home in 1938 when he was found to be suffering from tuberculosis, which took four years to cure. He then resumed his
education at Istanbul University, graduating in German
language and literature in 1950. For the next four years he was
an assistant in the history of art at the Faculty of Letters and
from 1954 he taught the same subject and the history of
literature in the Institute of Journalism of the Faculty of
Economics, while also teaching history of the theatre in the
Faculty of Letters. His first published story appeared in 1948.
He wrote for the newspaper *Tercüman* and was for a while its
editor. Although he was also a highly successful playwright, it
was for his short stories that he was most esteemed, and he is
still regarded by Turks as the greatest master of the genre.

GEOFFREY LEWIS, born in London in 1920, has degrees from
Oxford and an Honorary Doctorate of Bosphorus University,
Istanbul. Originally a classicist, his life was changed at the age
of eighteen when he chanced to leaf through an elementary
Turkish grammar. Since then he has spent his life studying and
teaching the language. (He is a Fellow of the British Academy,
Emeritus Professor of Turkish and Emeritus Fellow of St
Antony's College in the University of Oxford, and a Correspon-
ding Member of the Turkish Language Society.) His other
books include *Modern Turkey*, *Teach Yourself Turkish*, and a
translation of the Turkish national epic, *The Book of Dede
Korkut*.

THICKHEAD

and

other stories

Haldun Taner

THICKHEAD
and
other stories

by

HALDUN TANER

translated from the Turkish

by

GEOFFREY LEWIS

FOREST BOOKS/UNESCO
LONDON ☆1988☆ BOSTON

UNESCO COLLECTION OF
REPRESENTATIVE WORKS

European Series

These stories translated from Turkish have been accepted in
the translations collection of the United Nations
Educational, Scientific and Cultural Organisation (Unesco).

PUBLISHED BY
FOREST BOOKS

20 Forest View, Chingford, London E4 7AY, U.K.
P.O. Box 438, Wayland, MA 01788, U.S.A.

First published 1988

Typeset in Great Britain by Cover to Cover, Cambridge
Printed in Great Britain by A. Wheaton & Co Ltd, Exeter

Original Turkish text © Haldun Taner
Introduction and English translation © UNESCO 1988
Translated from Turkish by Geoffrey Lewis
Cover design © Janet Hart

British Library Cataloguing in Publication Data:

Taner, Haldun, 1915–1986
Thickhead and other stories.
1. Title
894'.3533 (F)

ISBN 0 948259 58 2

Library of Congress Catalogue Card No. 88–82588

Contents

Introduction	*ix*
To All Eternity	1
The Foot	9
The Vivid Green of the Leaf	33
It Works Both Ways	55
Ali Riza Efendi the Weighbridge Clerk	70
Morning by The Sea	80
The Statue	98
The Auction	105
Thickhead	123
No Trouble at All	143

Introduction

Haldun Taner was born in Istanbul in 1915, the son of Ahmet Selähattin, a lawyer who represented that city in the last Ottoman Chamber of Deputies. The discrepancy between the names of father and son is because it was not until 1934 that the adoption of surnames became a legal requirement for all Turks.

After completing his primary and secondary education at Galatasaray School, Haldun Taner studied economics and political science at Heidelberg, returning home in 1938 when he was found to be suffering from tuberculosis. It was during the long years of his cure and convalescence that he began writing, at first sketches for radio and then short stories, the first of which was published in 1948. He then resumed his education, reading German language and literature and the history of art at Istanbul University. From 1950 to 1954 he was assistant to the Professor of the History of Art at the Faculty of Letters, and then spent three years studying the theatrical arts in Vienna. On returning home, he taught the history of the theatre in the same Faculty, as well as lecturing on art and literature at the Institute of Journalism. He gave up teaching in 1972. All his short stories came out between 1948 and 1964. In the latter years his first play was produced and from then on he devoted himself to writing for the theatre.

The short story is the genre in which Turkish writers have most excelled since the 1930s. One possible reason for this is that during the decades of economic difficulty, when paper was scarce, it was hard to find publishers for full-length novels, whereas there was a steady demand for short stories from newspapers and magazines.

What set Haldun Taner apart from most of his peers and earned him the position, which he still holds after his death,

ix

as one of the most popular of all Turkish writers, was that he was never content merely to tell a good story. He had a gift for characterization and for dialogue. The people he presents to us, whether they be professors or waiters, doctors or policemen, all talk and act like their counterparts in real life. This of course helps to account for his great success as a writer of plays for the stage. But, more than that, he had a talent for seeing into the human heart and showing the thoughts that underlie actions and attitudes. It is not surprising that a man with so deep an understanding of human frailty and human strength should have had a highly developed sense of humour. Even in his most serious stories, such as the passionate *The Vivid Green of the Leaf*, the tragic *Thickhead*, and the macabre *The Foot*, there are moments of rich comedy. When he sets out to be funny, as in *The Statue* and *No Trouble at All*, he is very funny indeed.

It is a measure of his skill that his work can be enjoyed by non-Turks with minimal help in the form of annotation. Though the Turkish background will be unfamiliar to many readers, the stories are almost entirely self-explanatory. On the few occasions when a word of explanation has been thought necessary, it has been given at the beginning of the story.

English consonants have been used in the transcription of Turkish names. The Turkish vowels ö and ü (which have the same values as in German) have been retained, but not the undotted ı (which is pronounced like the i in 'cousin'). For the Turkish ğ, which generally has the effect of lengthening a preceding vowel, gh has been used. So Çamlıca appears as Chamlija, Hanım as Hanim, Şükrü as Shükrü, Germiyanoğlu as Germiyanoghlu.

The usual polite way of addressing or referring to people is to put the words Bey ('Lord') or Efendi ('Master') for men, and Hanim ('Lady') for women, after the first name: Gavsi Bey, Kiazim Efendi, Shükran Hanim. Turks habitually apply such kinship-terms as 'Brother' and 'Aunt' to people who are in fact not relatives, and even to strangers. Few instances of this practice have been retained in the English, as the translator's aim has been to avoid using folksy-sounding locutions which might give the reader pause. Thus Aghabey, properly 'Elder Brother,' has been translated as 'Guv' or 'Guv'nor.'

Geoffrey Lewis
Oxford

To All Eternity

[The Unionists referred to in this story and in *Ali Riza Efendi the Weighbridge Clerk* were the members of the Party of Union and Progress, which overthrew the tyranny of Sultan Abdulhamid in 1908, replaced it with a new tyranny and eventually brought the Ottoman Empire into the First World War, on the losing side. There were still quite a few of them around in 1948, when this story was written.]

What's the old saying? 'In the next world, grace; in this world, place.' If it weren't for Razi Bey, we'd never have had a place of our own. All these years I've been a schoolmaster. This is the year when I reach retiring age and till now we've never owned a house. Then Razi Bey goes and marries my wife's sister. He's a contractor, wide awake, pushful, enterprising. A previously undivided property on the outskirts of Ayvalik was being divided up. He managed to get hold of twelve acres of it at the price of agricultural land and with his two partners he's set up a housing co-operative. They're selling it off in plots to their friends and relations. None of the local worthies has even put in for one; they're the people who sit with their backs to the sea and reckon that for the wife and kids to go swimming would deprive the place of its virginity. Well, good luck to them; that's how we've managed to get a share. Naturally, the cooperative's houses will be built by Razi Bey and his partners and they'll make a bit on that too. I don't begrudge them. Every shareholder is being asked to put down a hundred thousand in advance, the balance to be paid off over six years at five hundred a month. It's a bargain, dirt cheap.

We've scratched around for cash. We've sold my wife's shop and my National Savings. We've got into debt but we've forked out the hundred thousand. The other shareholders haven't had to do that sort of thing; they're all well-off retired people. Razi Bey and his partners have got their

1

site organized and the building material is all stacked. Swarms of workmen have been brought in. They've started digging the foundations. So far, everything's fine. Then one morning the foreman looked in and said, 'There are some great big stones turning up in your plot.'

'Well, you'd hardly expect gold nuggets, would you? That's normal enough, isn't it?' I replied.

'These aren't just any old stones. Come and have a look.'

I did. Rectangular stones, one side flat, the other all knobs and bumps. 'Not important,' I said. 'Put them on one side: they may come in useful for the building.'

After he'd gone I thought I'd take an adze and give one of the stones a bit of a scrape. And what do you think I saw? A relief, a masterpiece. A big-bosomed woman clutching a child to her. Well, it's not surprising. Our Aegean coast is full of ancient works of art.

That evening I told my wife about it. 'These may be classical antiquities,' I said. 'We might show them to Shükran Hanim at the museum.'

'Oh come on! Don't make life more complicated!'

My wife has got it in for Shükran Hanim at the best of times, the way every woman who hasn't had an education feels about the woman who has, and has made a career for herself. Yet Shükran Tur is an inoffensive bit of a girl: short, skinny, silver-rimmed spectacles, never married nor likely to at this rate, with a degree in archaeology. Hardly opens her mouth. Doesn't smile much. Reads English books.

'What harm will it do if she sees them?' I said. 'What if they're antiquities?'

'And will you get a reward if they are?'

'I'd just like to do my duty as a civilized human being.'

That day I cleaned two more stones. A ceremonial procession: four people with offerings in their hands and sandals on their feet. Each of them more beautiful and full of expression than the last.

Early next morning, Razi Bey dropped in. 'I'll have some tea with you kids this morning,' he said. Never before had he dropped in like this. Without beating about the bush, he began, 'Well, Sunuhi Bey, I hear you've discovered some antiquities on your plot.'

I didn't like his mocking look. 'I'm just going to show them to Shükran Hanim, the director of the museum.'

'Shükran Tur's on leave. She's at Silifke. She'll be back at the end of the summer. Before that, at least let me have a look at them.'

I took him there. He saw them and turned them over and round. The mocking look vanished from his face and he frowned. 'Leave it,' he said. 'They're not antiquities. And suppose they were; would that be your business?'

'We'll just let Shükran Hanim see them.'

'You've got a fixation about letting Shükran Hanim see them. I mean, what'll happen if she does?'

'Isn't there such a thing as one's duty, one's duty to mankind, to civilization? What if they're the work of some great artist? What if they're a masterpiece, calling out from centuries past to centuries yet to come?'

'You say the weirdest things, Sunuhi Bey. Seeing they've been underground for centuries, where's the harm if they go on staying there?'

'But humanity . . .'

'Now you're starting on your humanity line. I'm not a complete clod, you know. You haven't mentioned this to anyone else, have you?'

'No.'

'Well, don't. In particular, that know-all Shükran Tur mustn't hear about it. Tell the labourers it turned out to be the floor of an old latrine. If any word gets out about antiquities, have you any notion of what will happen to us? The State will requisition the land and get excavations going. The property you got so cheap will be lost to you. The cooperative and all that will be over and done with. You and the rest of the shareholders will end up with nothing.'

'What you ought to be saying is that we have a choice between self-interest and duty.'

'Ah yes, duty. I knew that was coming. I've told you, don't make a thing of it, that's all.'

'May I remind you that I have always lived at peace with my conscience? The one thing I am proud of is my honour,

3

Razi Bey.'

My wife chimed in. 'Have you been excessively rewarded for your honourable service as a schoolmaster?'

Razi Bey added, 'We included you in our group because we thought you were a decent chap. Let's give him a stake in this nice little spot, we said. Are you going to make us regret it?'

'Please don't talk like that,' I said. 'I'm grateful that you've taken me into your group. I'm grateful all right but . . .'

'Come on, that's enough,' said Razi Bey. 'We all know you are honour incarnate. And the family are all proud of you. But this isn't just between the two of us. The interests of forty-seven shareholders are involved. One for all and all for one. If you don't keep your mouth shut, it's all done for; all the money and all the hope.'

When Razi Bey had gone, I said to my wife, 'Was it you who put him up to it?'

'What was I to do? I was afraid you'd go and do something crazy.'

'Well what do you think of that? This she calls crazy. Family matters ought to stay inside the family.'

'And is your brother-in-law an outsider?'

I had a rotten night and woke up in the morning with a headache.

'When a man gets to my age, what has he to live for? He lives to take things easy. Can someone with an uneasy conscience take things easy?'

'You've retired and you're still giving lectures. Stop being a bore!'

'Yes, maybe at first he lives to eat and drink and sleep. But when all that's taken care of, he aspires to other things. He lives to gain immortality. In order to be able to defy death, the poor devil has two possibilities open to him. Either he can have children and perpetuate his line, or he can compose immortal verses, like Sheykh Galib, or leave his mark on the world in some other way. And how is this done? It can be done with some masterpiece that calls out from centuries past to centuries yet to come. Why did the Pharaohs have the

Pyramids built? Why was the Tower of Babel reared to the skies? Why did Alexander and Napoleon set out to conquer the world? Why did Michelangelo do his statue of David? Why did Sinan the Architect build the Süleymaniye Mosque?'

'They all had a home to lay their heads in,' replied my better half. 'Have you ever owned a house till now? Cut out the rhetoric and stick to the facts. I'm in no mood to listen to you binding on, I've got a headache without that. If you're so keen, go and register as a guide and tell these stories to the German tourist women and those ugly brutes of German travellers with cameras.'

I could see I had more chance of being struck by lightning than of persuading her of the immortality of art, so I shut up. All night long I kept falling asleep and waking up. I dreamed about Phidias and Alexander the Great and Sinan the Architect. Funny thing was that Sinan didn't look a bit like the pictures of him in the art-history books.

My wife the mole must have been passing on everything that happened in the house, because next day I was accosted by that great hulking Nuri Iskeche and Sirri Erdem, the retired superintendent of police. Nuri Iskeche was breathing heavily through his nose. 'There's some daft gossip going round town,' he said. 'Or have some antiques really been found on the property of our cooperative, or what?'

I don't know if you've noticed, but these chaps just don't know the word 'antiquities'.

'I haven't said anything to anybody yet,' I said.

'Someone has, because people have heard about it.' After that he gave a long sigh. He shook his head from side to side perhaps ten times and muttered, 'God give me strength!' Then he said, 'If anyone mentions antiques again, I'm not kidding, there'll be bloodshed. We've put exactly fifteen million into this business. It's no joke.' He then looked me full in the face with his bloodshot eyes and said, 'Friend, I'm an old Union and Progress man: Razi may have told you. Yesterday in the café I swore an oath on my pistol.' And off he went. That's what's known as blackmail. Intimidation.

It turned out that Razi had been watching us from a

distance. He rushed up and took me by the arm. 'Pay no attention to Nuri,' he said. 'He's very hot-tempered. But you should have seen him yesterday in the café! If Sirri and I hadn't grabbed his hand he'd have fired his pistol. Well, after all, he is a former terrorist.'

'Who or what was he going to fire at? The reliefs, or their dead-and-gone artist?'

Sirri joined in the conversation. 'The important thing isn't Nuri's reaction but the interests of all of us. Don't you agree?'

Gavsi Bay, a retired member of the Council of State was, on the face of it, the most cultured man among them. At least he didn't call antiquities antiques. 'Anatolia,' he said, 'is like a layer-cake. In it there lie civilizations upon civilizations. All of them were built one on top of the other. Every city, every town, is like that. At one time a German Jew made off with the gold coins he'd got from the top layer of Troy and no one said a word. You know Istanbul, don't you? Istanbul. Wherever you put a shovel, Byzantium comes out from under it. You'll never build a house or a block of flats if you mean to go in for archaeological digs. You mustn't take these things so much to heart. What have they got to do with you?'

Razi too was very loquacious today. 'Where were you, Sunuhi, all those years when tribes of tourists were plundering these shores? Even the government turned a blind eye and now are you going to be the lone defender of the legacy of the past? Even Sultan Abdülhamid, do you know what he said? "If stones come out you can have them; if metal comes out it's mine."'

Now it was Sirri Erdem's turn. 'And, you know, people talk about a place being historical and all that, but it's just fables. Throughout history, so many civilizations have been founded, meant to last to all eternity, and then so many rulers emerged and demolished those civilizations, razed them to the ground and turned them into dust so that they in their turn could last to all eternity. The thing you call history is a vicious circle. My dear Sunuhi Bey, are you a shareholder in the cooperative or a conservator of historical monuments?'

They laughed. The odd thing is that I smiled too, not knowing what I was smiling at. Maybe it was just to show that I was still a party to the conversation, that I was not devoid of sophistication.

Three more days passed. Nuri Bey's terrorist pistol kept getting mixed up in my dreams. At the shareholders' meeting, new elections were held and I was chosen – God knows why – to be Treasurer. We heard that Shükran Tur, the museum director, had met an American at Silifke who'd got her a fellowship or something. She whizzed into town one evening and whizzed out again, then immediately shot off to Ankara to complete the paperwork. Sunk without trace.

Meanwhile it seems we have a visit from Razi Bey. My wife said to me one evening, 'Razi Bey wants the stones.'

'What does he think he's going to do with them?'

'How do I know? He said he was going to take them off in a lorry.'

'Where to?'

'Somewhere where they'd be safe,' he said. He had Gavsi Bey and Sirri Bey with him.'

About that time I had a serious inflammation of the kidneys and when I'd got over it I looked like Gandhi. Two months later the building work was finished. Thanks to Nuri Iskeche's intimidatory tactics, one didn't hear much talk in town about antiquities. Anyway, we're all going to be neighbours; there's no room for tension and ill feeling. As the saying goes, don't choose a house, choose a neighbour. Peace and harmony, that's the basic thing. All of us, how many days do we have as guests in this world? Recently, Sirri Erdem married off his daughter – may all our friends have the same good fortune. At the wedding there was eating and a great deal of drinking. When everyone was merry, Razi Bey, Nuri Iskeche and Gavsi Bey took me by the arm and we all embraced and kissed.

'We were on the point of falling out over nothing at all,' they said. 'Anyway, it's all over and forgotten.'

'It's true it's all over, but what I said wasn't wrong. What does man live for?'

'To be able to call out from centuries past to centuries

yet to come,' said my wife, in a fair imitation of my voice and way of speaking.

Razi Bey looked at Nuri Iskeche. Nuri Iskeche looked at my wife. Gavsi Bey said, 'Don't worry. Those masterpieces that call out from centuries past to centuries yet to come, we didn't throw them away or sell them or smash them into little bits. They're in a very secure place.'

'Where's that?' I asked.

'They're all in a very safe place; they're still looking to the centuries yet to come and calling out to them.'

'Where are they?' I asked.

Proudly Gavsi Bey replied, 'We used them to line the walls of the cooperative's septic tank.'

'What!' I roared. 'Shame on you!'

Gavsi Bey retorted, 'Now *you* are behaving shamefully. Credit us too with a modicum of respect for art, of intellect and right thinking. It would have been wrong for us to defile the faces of those lovely ancient reliefs with – you'll excuse me – our excreta. We turned them all backwards. Cheer up! Their faces are to the earth, they are still looking into eternity. They've turned their backsides to our septic tank – the backsides which in life they too used for excreting.'

'I give up,' I said. 'I mean . . .'

What else could I say?

Throughout my life, the expression 'I give up' has been the one I've used most often. It's only three syllables, it's easy to say and it does help relieve your feelings. Up to a point.

The Foot

[The Saar problem referred to in passing is the Franco–German dispute which began in January 1952 and was not resolved until October 1956, two years after the story was written. It will be noticed that the schoolchildren have numbers to identify them; a necessary practice, given the paucity of first names and the infrequent use of surnames in those days. The American auctions mentioned briefly in this story and more fully in *The Auction*, also written in 1954, were a feature of Istanbul and Ankara life at the time. Foreign currency being scarce and imports of non-essentials being restricted, sales of household goods by departing American service and business families attracted large numbers of eager buyers.]

Ihsan, who kept the slipper shop, threw two double sixes in succession and looked ready to go out with a gammon. He therefore pretended not to notice what Müslim was up to: shaking out a five and one and trying to pass it off as a five and two. He contented himself with murmuring, 'I threw a two and moved up three and still could not cheat destiny.'

Mesut Chaghlayan, the teacher at the primary school, was asleep, his legs extended like a huge letter V. A little way off, the café proprietor Salih was bent over, bringing out of the well the lemonade bottles he had hung in there not long before.

Salih's speckle-faced tabby must have liked the gurgling of the hubble-bubble, for she skipped about and then shot up onto the vet's lap. The vet had finished reading. He stroked the cat and folded the newspaper. The Saar problem was boiling up again. They hadn't yet been able to discover whose was the armless corpse that had appeared on the shore at Ahirkapi. It looked as though there was going to be another shortage of coke this winter. You really shouldn't read the paper. The more you did, the worse you felt.

Just as he was thinking this, along the dusty road that

9

stretched wearily out beneath the evening sun there came a pack of children, shouting and calling. The resident cat at once leaped to the ground and bolted into the empty pool. Mesut Chaghlayan awoke, mumbling. The back-gammon-players didn't even notice.

The child in front was dragging something tied to a string and the others were chasing him. The vet looked carefully over the top of his spectacles at what was being dragged, and shot out of his chair. 'Stop!' he shouted. 'Stop, I tell you!' But the children had long since turned the corner and vanished.

The vet turned to the others and called out, 'Grab them! Stop them, quick!' Mesut Chaghlayan, still fuddled with sleep, rushed over to his side. 'What's up, sir?'

All the vet could say was 'Foot'. He unbuttoned his collar and relieved the pressure on his neck, the veins of which were standing out. Then he said, 'Foot. That thing the children were dragging was a foot.'

Ihsan the slipper man and Muslim from the cookshop had abandoned their game and were listening, engrossed. The proprietor, bucket in hand, was staring.

'What foot?'

'A human foot.'

'What sort of foot?'

'An ordinary foot, my dear fellow. Cut off at the ankle.'

'Never!'

'Can't be, guv'nor.'

'So help me God. I swear to you. I saw it with my own eyes.'

'Well where did they get it from?'

'How do I know?'

Ihsan, scared that the game he was winning might go unfinished, said, 'My friend, if it's a foot it's a foot. It was found wherever it was found. Is it our worry? Come on, chum, let's see you throw those dice.'

Muslim quietly dropped the dice onto the table. 'Did you ever hear tell of such a thing? Wait a bit. What was it and what did it come off? Was it really a human foot they were dragging? Did you get a look at it, guv'nor? Could you have been mistaken?'

10

'Am I stupid?' Hark at him! Haven't I seen enough practicals in my time at anatomy lectures? That was an honest-to-God foot. A human foot. They'd threaded a string through the heel of it.'

'Good heavens!'

Mesut Chaghlayan, thoroughly awake by now, said, 'Where can they have found it?'

The vet picked his newspaper up from the table and put it in his pocket. 'The police must be informed,' he said. His decision was firm.

'What's it got to do with you?' shrieked Ihsan. 'Maybe they found it somewhere. The children didn't cut it off, you know.'

'Even so. Let's find out where they got it.'

The proprietor of the café said, 'One of the kids at the back was the son of the man we get our yoghurt from.'

'And where does your yoghurt man live?'

'Don't know.'

'Let's get going and find those children.'

The proprietor told the apprentice to look after the café. Ihsan was still obstinately refusing to budge, so they left him at his backgammon board and the rest of them started off down the road. By a lucky chance, on the way they ran into Inal, one of Mesut Chaghlayan's pupils. Seeing Mesut Chaghlayan coming towards him, the boy stuck his hands to his sides and stood to attention.

'A pack of children passed this way just now. Did you meet them?'

'Yes, teacher,' said Inal. 'They were dragging a foot after them. They'd bored a hole through the heel and threaded a string through it. A human foot.'

The vet turned to Müslim and gave him a look that meant 'Well?'

'Do you know those children?'

'Yes, teacher. They're from the Tin Can Quarter. We sometimes go to matches there.' He was on the point of adding, 'And once we had a fight with them over some mulberries,' but he didn't, for fear of annoying his teacher.

'Run and fetch whoever's at the police station. We'll be waiting here.'

11

In a little while Inal came running back. 'I told him,' he said, 'Sabri Efendi was there. He's 341 Erjan's father, in 4B. He's coming now.'

When 341 Erjan's father, in 4B, reached them he was puffing and blowing. He had asthma, and running wasn't good for him.

'What's happened, teacher sir?' he asked.

He had a special respect for Mesut Chaghlayan because he taught his son.

The matter was explained to Constable Sabri, by Mesut Chaghlayan.

Sabri said, 'First let's find the foot and take their statements. Then we'll inform the Public Prosecutor's office.'

When they arrived at the Tin Can Quarter, evening was falling and a cool breeze had sprung up. Oddly, although the upper branches of the apple trees were shaking and rustling, there was not a breath of wind in the lower branches. When the three ducks who were playing together in a mud-coloured swamp saw the men, they waddled hastily away.

The women were terribly agitated at seeing the policeman at the head of the procession. He marched on, without a word to them. The boys had disappeared as if by mutual consent. There were only three barefooted children beside a pile of debris. Two of them were playing dice; the third and smallest was busy trying to induce a grasshopper to smoke a cigarette.

At the sight of the policeman they made as if to run off, but were too late.

'Was it them, the ones you just saw?'

Inal said, 'That was one of them.'

Salih from the café said, 'The yoghurt man's son was there too.'

The policeman addressed himself to the freckled child whom Inal had indicated. 'All right, where's the foot?'

The child was breathing noisily. 'What foot, sir?'

The vet interrupted. 'He asks what foot and he . . . The foot you were dragging along just now, that foot.'

All three children replied in unison, 'We haven't seen a foot or anything. We don't know anything about it.'

But when the asthmatic policeman said, 'In that case, you come along to the station,' they owned up.

'It's Ibraam's, that foot. He found it. He won't let anyone have a go with it.'

'Who's this Ibraam?'

'His dad's Kiazim the builder. He's just gone with him to get sand.'

'What sand?'

'For the building.'

'What time will he be back?'

'All depends. Seven, eight, maybe half past.'

'Where has he put the foot, don't any of you know?'

'How are we to know, sir? He looks after it ever so careful. He never lets us play with it.'

Seven o'clock came, half past seven, eight, half past eight.

The policeman was close to exploding. Just as he was saying, 'Have you been having me on, you little . . .?' Ibraam turned up, on the sand-cart. He was a wizened boy, with tiny eyes and a very knowing face; he looked as though he had grown to maturity and then got small again. Inside the empty sand-cart, behind the huge horses, he was as big as a minute. It emerged that it had taken them some time to collect their money, because of a disagreement between the contractor and Bekir the master-builder. His father had gone on to Silivri in Bekir's truck and had sent him home wih the cart.

The large and fearsome-looking policeman planted himself in front of him and said, 'Bring out that foot, and quick.'

Ibraam was about to deny any knowledge of a foot, but he realized from the guilty look on his friends' faces that they had grassed on him. He had hidden the foot inside a broken jar in the stable, under the straw and the sacks. He went and brought it.

It was a piece of flesh, the colour of dried salt meat; at first sight, the fact that it was a foot was not all that obvious. One noticed two protruding bones at the severed ankle. Here and there were regions of white fat, as in butcher's meat. The

13

toes had gone thin and purple, and had shrivelled. Someone had bored a hole in the heel and passed a string through it.

'Where did you get this?'

'Over by the hospital, sir, on the rubbish dump.'

'What business have you there?'

'We go there every day to collect medicine boxes and streptomycin bottles. I found it there that day. Ali, the water-carrier's son, grabbed it out of my hand. We had a fight and I took it and ran off.'

'When did this happen?'

'Getting on for a fortnight.'

'Good,' said the policeman. 'Wrap it in a piece of paper.'

'Yes,' said Mesut Chaghlayan, 'find some paper. Greaseproof for preference.'

Ibraam's big sister ran off and somehow managed to get hold of some greaseproof paper. She was thinking that if she brought the greaseproof paper it might reduce her brother's punishment a bit.

Sabri Efendi the policeman addressed the gathering crowd. 'Come on, move along! It's not a show, you know!'

Mesut Chaghlayan felt sorry for the girl who had fetched the greaseproof paper and was now carefully wrapping the foot. 'I take it there's no need for the boy to come,' he said.

The vet and Müslim from the coffee shop were thinking that after all the foot had been found and it would be perfectly all right if the boy didn't come. Not Inal, of course; he wanted Ibraam punished.

The policeman insisted. Despite his particular respect for Mesut Chaghlayan, he said. 'Duty's duty, sir. He's got to come. His statement will be taken at the Public Prosecutor's office.'

Assurances were given by Müslim and Mesut Chaghlayan on behalf of Ibraam's sister. With the policeman in front, holding his precious trust wrapped in greaseproof paper, and the rest following, they set out for the Public Prosecutor's office.

By the time they reached the Law Courts, night had fallen. The duty Deputy Prosecutor had lit his pipe, put his plastic tobacco-pouch on the desk and, fountain pen in hand, was writing to his brother-in-law. When there was a knock on the door and the procession marched in, he was irritated. 'What's this crowd? What's going on?' he said and, turning to the policeman, added, 'I want them out of here. Tell me what the matter is, and be quick about it.'

The vet, Mesut Chaghlayan, Müslim, Salih, Inal, and Ibraam went out. The asthmatic policeman unwrapped the greaseproof paper, displayed the foot, and explained the problem from the beginning.

The Deputy Prosecutor looked at his watch and said, 'Very well, get on with it, take the boy's statement.'

Ibraam was brought in. The policeman wrote down what the boy had to say and got him to sign it. The Deputy Prosecutor finished the letter to his brother-in-law but could not find an envelope. Eventually he found one, put the letter in and stuck it down. Then he said to the policeman, 'Come on. We're going to the hospital.'

They went out together. The group waiting outside, full of curiosity, fell in behind them and they went downstairs.

The Deputy Prosecutor's motorcycle was just in front of the New Post Office, on the pavement where in the daytime the postcard seller displayed his wares. The Deputy Prosecutor took it down off the pavement and mounted it. The policeman, holding his precious trust, settled himself behind him. The Deputy Prosecutor tried to start it, but the engine didn't catch. He tried again, with the same result. At the third try it started. Drowning the quiet evening in uproar, the motorcycle flew off towards Ankara Avenue and was lost to view.

The duty Chief Assistant had taken off his glasses and was listening to the Deputy Prosecutor. The duty Chief Assistant was a literary buff as well as a doctor, of the school of Fahrettin Kerim, addicted to dropping appropriate lines of classical poetry at every opportunity, and convinced that he wielded his pen as elegantly as his scalpel. He was wild about the poetry of Yahya Kemal, and spent his spare time trying to match his quatrains. Indeed he had in front of him now a quatrain which he had just embarked on. He heard the Deputy Prosecutor out, breathing on his spectacles and polishing them. Then, putting them on again, he said, 'Impossible. There must be some mistake. As you are aware, no extremities or viscera excised in hospitals are thrown onto a dump or just given to the dustman or anything like that. Some are incinerated within the hospital. Others are destroyed, without being shown to anyone, by special sanitary teams.'

The policeman said to himself, 'How dreadful! That means they're burnt in the furnace. What a shocking thing! Imagine how the flesh must sizzle!'

The Deputy Prosecutor, like all deputy prosecutors, was a man of intelligence. 'Hm!' he said. 'In that case, it must have been left there on purpose. Simply to give the impression that it had been thrown from this building. By someone unacquainted with hospital regulations, of course.' To which he added, with a smile, 'Like me.'

The duty Chief Assistant politely corrected him. 'Like everybody.' For some moments he had been picking the foot up and laying it down again. He now stood it upright.

Silence fell in the room. There was only the humming of the ventilator, which was on although the weather was cool, and the harsh breathing of the asthmatic policeman.

The Deputy Prosecutor shook the ash of his cigarette off into the ashtray and said, 'There is another problem. Recently there's been a man cutting off the arms and legs of his victims and leaving them lying about. You may have read about it in the papers. Last week we found an armless corpse on the shore at Ahirkapi. It may well be that this is the work of the same monster.'

The duty Chief Assistant, who wanted to get back to his quatrain as soon as possible, was on the point of saying, 'That is no concern of mine,' but he refrained, saying instead, 'It is possible.' And as he pronounced these words he at once realized that it was scarcely possible. The toes of the foot in particular were displaying the purplish wrinkling peculiar to gangrened members. Both for that reason and because at that moment the frothy coffee had arrived, he said, to please the Deputy Prosecutor, 'Nevertheless, to be on the safe side, let me have it looked into. Yes, certainly.'

The Deputy Prosecutor said, 'Please do. I shall be obliged to you. If it isn't a trouble, of course.' The duty Chief Assistant's hair being somewhat sparse, he supposed him to be at least an associate professor.

The duty Chief Assistant pressed the bell. 'Please!' he said. 'How can it be a trouble? It's our duty.'

'You make me quite ashamed.'

'I beg of you!'

The duty Chief Assistant said to the sister who came in, 'Saime Hanim, will you ask Selman Bey to come and see me?'

At that moment Selman Atajan was stretched out on his bed, reading Churchill's memoirs. When the sister came in and told him he was wanted by the duty Chief Assistant, it dawned on him what he was wanted for. Selman Atajan, like all new surgical assistants, was an extremely nervous young man. Wouldn't it just be his luck if the tram-driver, whose appendicitis he had not made a good job of the day before, had developed symptoms of peritonitis, or if the school-teacher from whose thyroid he had taken quite a deep cut the previous week should show signs of tetanus?

When he went in and learned what the problem actually was, he brightened up enormously. Moreoever, it turned out that he and the Deputy Prosecutor knew each other; they had been at the same primary school when Selman Atajan's father was Sub-Governor of Nallihan. Ah, the good old days! How quickly time passes!

As to the question of whether or not he had amputated the foot, no, he hadn't amputated any feet lately. In fact, in all his life he had only performed one such operation. That had been four months ago, and it wasn't at the ankle but below the knee. Nor was it a left leg, but a right leg, he rather thought. 'Besides,' he said, 'it's curious that it should have been found on the dump. Because no extremities or viscera excised in hospitals are . . .'

'Of course, of course. They are incinerated or destroyed in a special way. *I* know that.'

The Deputy Prosecutor winked and smiled at the Chief

Assistant as he said this. The Chief Assistant smiled back. They smiled together. Selman Atajan thought they were making fun of him, and became a little sulky, but when the Deputy Prosecutor explained what they were smiling at he smiled too. In short, the atmosphere of the room became very cheerful. So much so, that one might have expected the Chief Assistant to recite a line of classical poetry appropriate to the situation. He didn't, though. On the contrary, suddenly turning serious, he asked, 'Very well, what do we do now?'

Selman Atajan said, 'Let's just ask Iskender Iskit.'

'Is Mr Iskender on duty tonight?' The Chief Assistant had given the 'Mr' a special emphasis, thus conveying mockery and disparagement. He believed that by calling people he did not like 'Mr' he was taking a kind of revenge on them. This was not reprehensible; it was a question of temperament. He did not like Mr Iskender Iskit. The fellow had been lucky enough to play his cards right and do an eight-month attachment in London. Now his conceit was intolerable and he considered himself superior to the associate professors and full professors.

Outside his profession, this Iskender's sole interest, or, to use his favourite English term, hobby, was photography. Indeed, he was now talking about photography to the assistant radiologist, who had dropped in to visit him. 'Have you ever done pictures at night with Promicrol?'

'No never. Have you?'

'I recently took some pictures in the street in Beyoghlu, at one-fiftieth, with an f/stop of 3.5. I washed it for fifty-five minutes. You'd be astonished. All the details were there. No grain, nothing.'

'Extraordinary. But your camera's an Exacta, isn't it?'

'No, it's a Rolleiflex. Is yours a reflex?'

'I sold that one, getting on for a month ago. Now I've a Retina 2. Zeiss Tessar lens, 1:3.5.'

'Are you pleased with it?'

'Its great drawback is that you can't take the film out until you've shot all thirty-six.'

'Then cut it yourself, cut it at the tenth frame.'

'My dear fellow, one doesn't always have access to a dark

room. I do my developing in the bathroom. Another fault with these miniature films is that they're not suitable for big enlargements.'

'Use a fine-grain bath, you'll get your enlargements. Wash it in Formula D.K.20. Then you'll be able to blow it up to thirty by forty, even fifty by sixty.'

When the sister knocked at the door, that ended the conversation.

Iskender Iskit was annoyed that the Chief Assistant had sent for him at such an inconvenient time. He went in with a cross expression on his face. The problem was explained to him. He listened to the story. He took the foot, turned it in every direction, put it down, picked it up. 'No,' he said, 'I can't possibly have amputated this.'

'How can you be so sure?' asked Selman Atajan.

Whereupon Iskender Iskit laughed. But it was not a genuine happy laugh; it was a nervous, hysterical laugh. When he laughed, one could see the wires which the dentist had put on in order to straighten his teeth. 'It's very simple, my friend,' he said. 'In this type of amputation I cut the fibula a little shorter than the tibia, so that the stump takes a conical shape and makes a more comfortable fit in the prosthesis.' He then looked at the Chief Assistant and Selman Atajan, with a look which implied, 'Have you taken that in?' It wasn't just in the look; in the way he stood, and in the words whose echoes were still ringing in the room, one could detect the overwhelming superiority conferred on him by his eight months in London.

The asthmatic policeman said to himself. 'I'm blowed if I understood a word of all that. Still, it's no business of mine. The young fellow did speak nicely. You can always tell an educated man. I wonder if I ought to get these people to take a look at my asthma while I'm here?'

'Very good,' said the Chief Assistant, 'thank you.'

'Nicely done!' thought Iskender Iskit, enormously pleased to see the Chief Assistant put out. 'Stand up for yourself a bit, and get with it!'

Selman Atajan, who sensed all these cross-currents, pointed to the foot and said, 'You mean this wasn't

19

amputated with your technique.'

The intelligent Deputy Prosecutor rather fancied that in the mocking tone of this remark he detected a toadying eagerness to please the Chief Assistant. 'Are the assistants always getting at one another like this?' he wondered. 'Just like us and the judges. What's obvious is that this young fellow is better than the other two; they can't stand it and so they try to make fun of him. I can see why he didn't lose his cool.'

The asthmatic policeman was feeling uncomfortable because of the chain-smoked cigarettes and he had begun to make as if to leave. If only they had the sense to open a bit of window!

To relieve the tension in the room, and to make the atmosphere more friendly, the Deputy Prosecutor said, 'So our friend here didn't amputate it either. That means it wasn't amputated in this hospital.'

He was just getting ready to apologize and go, when in came the duty Theatre matron, Müsherref Mutlu. Her surname meant 'Happy', but, bless her, she never smiled. But the poor thing couldn't help it, she had chronic rheumatism. That was why she came lurching in like an old woman, though she was only forty-five.

The policeman was astonished at the sight of her. How could a person be in a hospital, amongst all these doctors, and not find a remedy for what ailed her?

Müsherref Mutlu's eyes moved from the foot standing on a table to the Deputy Prosecutor and finally came to rest on the Chief Assistant. When the latter briefly explained what the matter was, she said, 'Haven't you asked Erjüment Bey?'

Selman Atajan hastily intervened. 'For goodness sake, Erji is on leave, isn't he? He's on his honeymoon, didn't you know?'

'That's as may be,' she replied. 'Before he went on leave he amputated a foot, unless I'm much mistaken.'

She seemed really pleased at the idea of disturbing the honeymooning doctor.

The Chief Assistant asked, 'Do you have a telephone

number for him?'

'I must have.'

'I'm sorry to bother you but please find it for me quickly.'

Iskender Iskit had been on the point of leaving, but he lingered. He was now intensely curious to know the outcome.

Selman went to the telephone and dialled the number. His eyes on the foot in the greaseproof paper, he began to wait.

When the phone rang Erji was in the lavatory. His wife had put on her kimono, and was reclining on the sofa, one leg over the other, studying the new style of wall appliqués in the latest number of *Home Journal*. She was very well up on matters relating to furnishing and interior decorating, or so she thought. She it was that had found this single-storeyed house resembling a Swiss chalet, she that had chosen the furniture, approved the curtains and coverings, and had the walls painted in this hazelnut green. Erji didn't count for much, except in bed. The man who marries a daughter of rich parents must to some extent put up with this.

'Allô!' she said, in a French accent, not 'Hallo!' Had she confined herself to saying 'Allô,' she could have been taken for a Parisienne. 'Allô!' she said. 'Is it Erjüment you want? He can't come at the moment, he's in the bathroom. Let me just see if he's out yet.' She then turned towards the lavatory and called, 'Erji! Erji!'

Erji had just finished what he had to do and came at a run. 'What's up, sweetie?'

'It's the hospital. They want you.'

'At this hour of night? Let me have it.'

On taking the telephone, Erji suddenly became the complete surgeon. 'What do you say? A left foot, cut off at the ankle? Yes. That is correct. Honestly, I can't tell you whether it was a right or a left foot, but I did indeed cut off a foot like that. Getting on for three weeks now. How am I to know, dear boy? A fisherman, a boatman; something of that sort. For heaven's sake, is one to be disturbed at midnight over this? Show it to the patients in the wards; the owner will certainly recognize it. That's if he hasn't been discharged, of course. No, no, my dear fellow, I hadn't gone to bed yet. Eh? Yes. What was that again? No. Very well. Goodbye. I'll tell her; thank you my dear fellow.'

His wife put her arms round Erji's neck. 'What is it, darling? What is it?'

'Nothing, sweetest. Selman sends you his regards.'

'What was he calling you about? For God's sake, what is it, that cut-off foot?'

'An amputation, my dolly.'

She had suddenly become agitated. Breathlessly she asked, 'Has there been a complication? They're not holding *you* responsible, are they?'

'No, my dolly. Do I have complications in my operations?' He smiled, because he had had some difficulty in enunciating this infelicitous sentence. 'An amputated foot has been discovered and they think it was thrown out of the hospital. Apparently what they want to find out is whether it was us who amputated it.'

'Oh I feel awful!' said the young bride. Indeed, she had gone deathly pale. Although she was a surgeon's wife, she could not look at an open wound, and the sight of blood made her feel faint. Given that she had this interest in interior decoration, she would have done far better to marry an architect, but it was not to be. Kismet. What else was there to say? In time she would get used to it. 'So what did you tell him? How will they find out whose it was?'

'I told them to take it round the wards and ask.'

'Well done, darling!' She sneaked a glance at the mirror, to see if her perm had been spoilt. Erji had come to the telephone a minute or two ago without washing his hands. He now went and washed them. Then, locked in a close embrace, they sat on the sofa. She found in *Home Journal* a table very much like the three-legged, ash-coloured one which she had unsuccessfully attempted to describe to her husband, and showed it to him. A similar one had been sold at the American auction the week before, for three hundred and fifty liras. The couple made their minds up. This Sunday they would go to the auction at the Chamlibel Apartments in Nishantash.

Those assembled in the Chief Assistant's room were at a loss what to do. Selman Atajan said, 'There's nothing for it but to take Erji's advice: show the foot to the patients and ask them.'

'And supposing the owner of it has been discharged? After all, it's three weeks now.'

'He won't have been discharged.'

'Let's just ask.'

'No, let's not.'

'What do we stand to lose?'

'That's true enough; let's ask.'

It was agreed. In the lead, holding the foot, went Matron. Behind her came the Chief Assistant and the Deputy Prosecutor. Behind them was Müsherref Mutlu, and after her the policeman, Iskender Iskit and Selman Atajan. They began to go round all the wards, one by one.

When the procession reached Ward Three, most of the patients were preparing to go to sleep. The ward orderly, seeing them in the corridor, supposed that the Deputy Prosecutor was a minister or an inspector. He ran ahead of him and, as though he had only now managed to find time amid all his work, grabbed a duster and started busily polishing the floor.

The interior of the ward smelt of phenol. This smell affected the policeman, and he held his handkerchief to his nose.

One elderly patient who looked like a Tijani dervish, the ends of his beard yellowed, strand on strand, was standing on his bed, performing the ritual of the night prayer.

The only patient in this ward who had undergone an operation on his foot was Shahin from Rize, on the Black Sea, who was in bed number twelve. He was asleep with his face to the wall, dead to the world. Although it was three weeks since his operation he had not yet been discharged, having been found to have an excess of sugar. He had pulled the blanket up to his head and was dreaming of the days when he was fit and well.

Matron gave the bed a gentle shake. He took no notice. She prodded his shoulder; this time he opened his eyes.

23

Heavy with sleep as he was, he could not understand what was going on. He looked round him in a stupor. Seven pairs of eyes were regarding him fixedly. What was wrong? And there was a policeman amongst them too.

A voice: 'You had an operation on your foot.'

He looked. It was the Chief Assistant.

'That's right,' he said. As he spoke, his left ankle throbbed with sudden pain.

'Gangrene, was it?'

'That's what they reckoned, God damn them.'

The Chief Assistant, edging in front of Matron so as to conceal the foot, broached the question in what he fondly imagined was a tactful way. 'Who performed your operation?'

'Pulent, was it, or Ejmet? Some posh name like that.'

'It must have been Erjüment Bey.'

'Jolly good, that's it!' That was what he said aloud, but inside he was indignantly wondering what the idea was of waking a man up in the middle of the night and asking him all these questions. He suddenly felt as if his heart was being crushed. It was as if he had only just noticed that for three weeks there had been no foot attached to his left ankle. How nicely he had forgotten all that had happened! Would you believe it, this fellow was going to make him tell the whole story all over again!

But the Chief Assistant did not make him do that. 'And now you're all right, eh?'

'Aye, I'm all right, thank God.'

'I suppose you were nearly asleep?'

'I had just dropped off.'

'Now look, friend, there's a bit of a problem. This gentleman here is the Deputy Prosecutor . . .' Then, finding this preamble much excessive, he blurted out, with no further attempt at tact, 'Just take a look at this, maybe you'll recognize it. Is it your foot?'

As Matron suddenly moved away from in front of him, the Rize man's eyes were all at once confronted with the sight of a lump of flesh, the colour of salted meat. His face went green. He was revolted. Covering his eyes with both hands, he turned away. 'I shan't look at it,' he told himself, 'Nothing will make me look at it.'

They all looked at each other. The Deputy Prosecutor leaned over the bed. 'Shame on you!' he said, 'I should never have expected it of a man like you. You're keeping us all waiting. Come on, look at it and tell us.'

Once his manliness had been called in question, the man from Rize could have looked even through the gate of Hell. Slowly he turned to his left. He brought his emaciated hands down from his eyes. Reluctantly he looked once more at the foot. And now he kept his eyes on the foot, without a word.

This foot, aye, this foot. He looked at it carefully. This foot was his foot. Could he fail to recognize it? All right, but why had they threaded that string through the heel? He closed his eyes, then opened them again.

This foot, aye, this foot. So never again would he tread on the moist sand with this foot, and dry its damp sole in the warm pebbles. So never again would he give this foot a good scratch when there were chilblains between the toes. Never again would this foot roam over Hajer's calves in bed.

All at once he felt himself lost, as though he had been deprived of his manhood. Would a man who could not stamp his left foot hard on the ground ever be considered a real man? And how ashamed Hajer would be of her crippled husband! Never in his life had Shain feared death, but he had dreaded the thought of living as an invalid. Now what he had dreaded had happened. And it seemed as if it had happened to him not three weeks ago, at the operation, nor yet a month before that, when his foot became gangrenous, but now, at this very moment.

Idris's fiddle was loud in his ears. At Rize, when they were stamping round in the *horon*, when they were dancing *Alika* or *Memetina Papilat*, Shahin was the best of all. He would dance for half an hour at a stretch, an hour, an hour and a half. Without stopping to rest, without tiring, without growing weary of it. Gradually warming up and coming to the boil, shouting 'Come on lads, Come on!' to bring them to the heights of exaltation. A vast array of buskined feet came before his eyes. Idris was playing and they were all dancing the *horon*, widening and narrowing the circle, stretching and shrinking, swaying and straightening up. At last came the moment when there was only one pair of buskins left in the dance, and you cannot have a *horon* with only one pair of dancing buskins. 'Stop the fiddling, friend Idris!'

From now on, he reflected, he would only have one shoe to get cleaned. Who would he give the other one to? But his shoulders, neck, and arms were fine. Perfectly sound. He would press against the footboard with his good leg and he could still row. He seemed to see himself in the boat, rowing. Every time he pulled on the oars, the thole-pins would creak, but so too would the wooden foot as he put his weight on it.

'Do say, brother, this foot, is it yours? What are you dreaming about?'

So from now on he would walk bobbing up and down like the waves in the south wind. In the quarter where he lived there was a one-legged child. The poor little chap, so as not to be behind the others, tried to play football with his wooden leg, hopping along like a grasshopper. The man from Rize suddenly realized that now, when he thought he was feeling sorry for that boy, he was feeling sorry for himself.

'He can't have recognized it, he can't. Maybe it's not his.'

The children on the shore would no longer want to get into his boat. A blonde girl, her hair the colour of meerschaum, would tug at her nurse's hand and say, 'Nanny, let's not get in that wooden-legged man's boat. If we overturn he won't be able to save us.' And she would lead the woman off in the direction of Rizik's boat. It was true; could anybody swim with a wooden leg? All right, let's suppose he could; and what about when he was bringing in the boat? When you did that, you just threw your right foot onto the quay, and hooked the big toe of this left foot onto the edge of the boat. He looked at the amputated foot in Matron's hand. That thick, powerful big toe was now thin, shrivelled, deep purple in colour, and drooping.

'Shahin Efendi, why are you so lost to the world? What are

26

you thinking so hard about?'

What odd things were coming into his head. The examination they had to take for flat feet when he joined the Navy. They made each of them put his feet into a bucket of water and then walk barefooted. From the damp footprints on the deck they could tell the ones who had flat feet. If this examination were done now, he thought, he would leave on the deck, alongside the print of a sound right foot, the print of a round wooden foot with a rubber ferrule.

He lowered his head and looked at the feet of the people in front of him. They all had two each. The shoes of the man they called the Deputy Prosecutor were newly polished, gleaming. The policeman had boots on. The Chief Assistant had moccasins. One of the other assistants had come down in slippers. The Matron's white linen shoes had buckles on top. She had legs like stovepipes, straight up and down. Usually, when he saw her lurching round the ward, he felt sorry for her, thinking, 'Poor woman, and she's not even old yet'. But he didn't feel sorry for her now. They might look like stovepipes, they might look like anything at all, but she had two complete legs, hadn't she? They might hurt all the time, but the woman had two legs. What did it matter if they were rheumatic and looked like stovepipes?

'Say, will you? Is this foot yours? Haven't you recognized it yet?'

From the Rize man's grey-blue eyes, tears descended in a steady stream. He gulped, his Adam's apple bobbing up and down. Then he groaned, 'It's mine. This foot's mine, mine, mine.'

Out of respect for his grief, for a moment they were all silent. And, as is usual when people are touched, they gazed into the far distance. The Chief Assistant found ten seconds of silence adequate and he asked, in a voice which tried to be gentle, 'Very well, and how do you recognize it?'

'There you are, you see, my little finger and the one next to it are stuck together, same as my toes.'

The Chief Assistant and the Deputy Prosecutor bent down and looked. True enough, the man's little fingers and ring fingers were joined, from the root to the middle. He brought his sound leg out from under the quilt. This muscular right foot had big protuberant bones, the purple veins of it bulged, and the little toe and its neighbour were joined at the base, like those of the left foot.

The Chief Assistant and the Deputy Prosecutor looked overjoyed. They exchanged happy glances. Matron too seemed to be happy at their happiness; she was looking at them and smiling.

The Chief Assistant turned to the man from Rize. 'Good night, skipper,' he said. 'Sorry we had to bother you.'

'Go in good health,' he replied, his voice still husky and indistinct.

The Chief Assistant and the Deputy Prosecutor walked towards the door, and the others followed. Occasional snores had begun to rise up in the ward. The sparsely-bearded dervish type was now squatting cross-legged on his bed, holding a mineral-water bottle and looking at them.

The hospital clock struck the hour.

The man from Rize was lying on his back, his eyes on the ceiling, thinking. Every so often he tugged at his nose.

It was now incumbent on Matron to ascertain how the foot had come to be thrown onto the dump. She took it on herself to carry the investigation on from here. First she talked to the ward sisters, then she went to the orderlies' dormitory and interrogated one or two of them. It did not take her long to collar the culprit.

It was a man from Kastamonu, called Süleyman. In his first week at the hospital he had been assigned to surgical, but he couldn't take it, and had been transferred. On the day when the man from Rize was operated on, they had brought Süleyman back because the regular theatre orderly was on leave. He went through a terrible time as the surgeons were cutting and hacking away. When the operation was over and Erjüment, heedless of whether this was the usual man or a new one, handed him the bloody severed foot, Süleyman's head swam and he almost threw up. Having no idea of where extremities or viscera cut away during operations were supposed to be taken, he threw the foot out of the first

28

window he came to, straight onto the dump.

The Deputy Prosecutor folded the deposition which he had got the policeman to take, and put it in his pocket. He thanked the Chief Assistant again and shook him by the hand. Then he gave a pat on the back to Selman Atajan, his classmate from the Nallihan primary school, and said, 'I'll expect you to come and see us at home one of these days. And be sure to bring your father. I live in Kalamish, in Sait Pasha Street. We have a bit of a garden. We don't spend anything on vegetables. I'll let some bottles of beer down into the well, we'll put out the reclining chairs, and we'll have ourselves a party and talk about old times.'

They settled it. One Sunday, Selman would collect his father, the former Sub-Governor of Nallihan, and go to Kalamish. The address was written down. A sketch-map was drawn on the back of a cigarette packet. Then the Deputy Prosecutor once more put the policeman behind him and sat down in the saddle. He went through the motions of starting the engine and it did not catch. He tried again, with the same result. At the third try, it caught. But they were not yet moving off. The policeman had felt something was missing from his hand. It seemed to him that they had forgotten something.

'The foot,' he said. 'We've forgotten the foot.'

His words, however, were lost in the roar of the engine. He prodded the Deputy Prosecutor and asked, 'What's going to happen to the foot, sir?'

The Deputy Prosecutor, shouting amid all the noise, and smiling at the Chief Assistant, said, 'It will be disposed of in whatever way all extremities and viscera excised in hospital are disposed of.'

On account of the noise, the Chief Assistant had not been able to hear what was said but as he could tell from the Deputy Prosecutor's manner that he had just fired off another witticism, he smiled politely.

The policeman said to himself, 'Dammit, I was going to ask for something for my asthma, and I didn't get round to it. But it wouldn't have been suitable, not with the Deputy Prosecutor there and all. Never mind, eh? I've got to know

29

the doctors, after all. They're all good chaps, and some other time I'll get them to take a look at me.'

The Deputy Prosecutor put his motorcycle into gear, with the happy feeling of having concluded the matter with a good joke. In the roar of the engine, Justice and Police departed from the hospital.

The Chief Assistant had come out as far as the gate and was looking at them as they sped down the road. 'It's downright cold of an evening,' he thought. 'Winter's coming.' He lit a cigarette and went inside. Since his inspiration took wings in the evening hours, he was impatient to return to the quatrain he had begun not long before the Deputy Prosecutor's arrival. He sat down at the desk, vainly trying to recall the rhyme he had hit on and then forgotten. His failure to recall it irritated him. He thought for a while, his eyes on the picture of Jemil Pasha that hung on the wall. Finally he collected up his draft notes and went to bed.

Selman Atajan had returned to his room and resumed his reading of Churchill's memoirs. Churchill was telling how his life had been saved thanks to penicillin, and how, in the most critical time of the Second World War, he had relaxed by painting in North Africa. Selman Atajan said, 'Terrific chap, this Churchill. How cross Erjüment was when we telephoned! I wonder what the dirty dog and his wife were up to. My dad will be very pleased to see the Deputy Prosecutor. If I were to take my bathing costume, we might go to the Fenerbahche beach. I didn't look at his hand, I suppose the lad's married. If so, I must take his wife some sweets from Lebon's shop.'

Matron had found someone to whom she could give a thorough dressing-down, and her pleasure knew no bounds. All her life was spent in looking for opportunities like this. The only nights on which she managed to get to sleep without taking Bromural were those when she could find some wretch on whom to vent all her fury.

She could not be blamed for this; she was an hysteric. In her youth she had married an accountant. He was carrying on with the neighbour's sister-in-law and eventually ran away from home. Thereafter she bore all men a grudge, and now she took it out on the patients and the orderlies.

Süleyman from Kastamonu, head bowed like one condemned to death, was looking at the toes of his shoes. 'Come along with me,' she said, 'I'm going to tell you a thing or two.' And in a wrath which made her forget her rheumatism she marched straight to her office.

Once the owner of the foot had been discovered, Iskender Iskit had not waited for any more but had gone up to his room. Finding it empty, he hurried off to the assistant radiographer's room. After he had briefly explained why he had been called down, they returned to their discussion. Now they were on fixing-baths. Iskender said, 'I add metabisulphite to the hypo. It fixes the film well and it prolongs the life of the bath, which doesn't get dirty so quickly.'

'You're absolutely right,' replied the other. 'And in summer you should use alum. It stops the film melting.'

As for Erjüment and his wife, they were now preparing for bed. They had made it their custom to drink a glass of cognac each before retiring. In order to prevent the sexual disharmony common in newly-weds and to adapt his fiancée to his ways as soon as possible, he had followed the example of all his doctor friends and given her a German sex manual very early on, and it had proved most beneficial.

As she threw off the slippers with the pom-poms and got into bed, the expensive spring mattress, purchased at yet another American auction, gave a well-bred creak.

Once the Deputy Prosecutor and the policeman had left and the assistants had gone off to their rooms, the hospital returned to its normal state.

The old night watchman was winding his clock at the control socket in the corridor.

Matron, tired out with telling Süleyman off, washed her feet in hot water and her flushed face in cold, and went to bed.

Süleyman's neighbour in the orderlies' dormitory made

fun of him for a full hour.

And all through that night, till morning, the left foot of the man from Rize hurt and hurt, as though it were still there.

The Vivid Green of the Leaf

[Two points in this story call for an explanation. The name Zuhal, by which the heroine likes to be known, is rather fancy, whereas her real name, Hamide, is more down-to-earth. And the reason for her calling the Goethe Institute 'the Bum Institute' is that the first syllable of 'Goethe' sounds embarrassingly like the Turkish for 'anus'.]

The boat is gliding like oil over the dark sea, neither fast nor slow, at a constant speed, as if moving of its own accord, emitting a slight plopping sound from its prow.

As the oars go back, they sway up as if licking the water. They dip with a compassionate softness, as if caressing the sea for fear of startling it into wakefulness. As they quietly emerge from the water, sketching lines of phosphorescence in front of them, the two or three drops shed from their tips, seemingly in accord with the plopping sound in front, accentuate the cosmic peace of a gentle, healthy pulse-beat. Then as they sway back once more they move into that soft, affectionate plunge. How beautifully one might sleep to the lullaby of this rhythm. In the voice of the girl facing me there is the mist of drowsiness, but in her eyes, which she opens as big as saucers, there is a monstrous surprise.

'Still, you row very well, dear,' she says.

The first time she has called me 'dear'.

Another odd thing: starting her sentence not with 'I see' but with 'still'. Why does she have to cast a shadow with that 'still' even over the fact that she has detected some merit in me? So that I shouldn't get above myself. And in that 'still' there is also this overtone: Seeing that you row so gently, seeing that you have the power to bring me to a state very close to drunkenness, on a night with no moon and no poetry, simply by the way you row so quietly, why do you have to be such a pedant, such a jaw-me-dead, such a know-all?

I ask you, look at her choice of words. 'Still, you row very well, dear.' She is the most pedantic of pedants.

Pelit's is an attractive café in Beyoghlu, just opposite the
Tepebashi Theatre. It is frequented mostly by the bearded,
pipe-smoking writer, artist, and thinker set and the actors,
opera-singers and musicians from the theatre across the road.
Seyfettin Chürüksulu, the lovable Maecenas of the day, calls
it 'The Café Grössenwahn', because of the similarity he sees
in it to the Café des Westen in Berlin. That too, it seems, was
a haunt of arty people and that is why it was known as the
Café Grössenwahn, 'Bighead'. By likening Pelit's to that
place he succeeds in casting himself back into his youth, into
the midst of his memories of his younger days. There is good
reason why this café is popular with those who have a
smattering of German culture. Both the waiters know
German. They answer to 'Herr Ober!' And the place makes
the loveliest Apfelkuchen.

That explains why this is the favourite resort of several of
the most emancipated students of the German and Austrian
Lycée and of the German Philology Department of the
University. I think it's like the Viennese cafés. In Vienna,
every writer has his Stammcafé, his regular café, in which he
has his Stammtisch, his regular table. There he reads, there
he writes and there he receives interviewers. Why shouldn't
the table by the window be my Stammtisch? You cannot get
away from the fact that I am, or, to be more accurate, that at
that time I was, a writer whose newly-burgeoning stories
sometimes came out even in German magazines.

Writers, you know, have fertile imaginations and they
sometimes weave myths not only about their heroes but
about themselves too. They create an image of what they
want to be, what they wish to resemble. Then they try to
conform to it, after their fashion. When they fancy that they
do conform to it, they are delighted. To see signs of it in
someone else's mirror burnishes their self-esteem. Which of
us has not gone through these foolish phases in our youth?
But some keep up this buffoonery all their lives. They are the
incorrigible fools. In some it doesn't last so long; it's an
infantile disorder like scarlet fever or measles. A year, or
five, or ten. Then people, events, and frustrations abrade

him and the day comes when he wearies of this game. He realizes that it is more comfortable, less tiring, to be as one is. He begins to be an adult.

At the period I'm talking about I suppose I had not got past that stage. Far from my balloon's being punctured, unfortunately my circle were inflating it.

I was a great success with the female lectors of the Goethe Institute, the girl undergraduates in Philosophy and German Philology, the senior class of the German Lycée and several of the German au pairs. They would come up and ask a question. If I invited them to sit down they would at once do so. Some would set out their thoughts about one of my articles, some would openly ask for help with their philosophy essays, and they would get it. Especially if they were beautiful I would never turn them away. Beauty is God's greatest gift to mankind. Even when it is unaccompanied by any good qualities. Who, at that age, doesn't enjoy being listened to attentively by the girls who surround him, young, beautiful, and bright of eye?

At that time I was young, a bachelor and as free as a bird. I fancied that I was collecting material for future use from every incident that chanced my way. Add to that the fact that I was assistant to one of the professors at the University. And that I had picked up from the foreign teachers a soft tone of voice – yes, a soft tone of voice because people of culture always speak softly – and elegant movements of the hands, arms, and head. More important, I had picked up the habit of not engaging in small talk. Whenever I talk, it is on subjects about which I really and truly know something and have been through some books. The girls leave, and I light a Dutch cigar and start reading my *Weltwoche* or my *Theater Heute*. Sometimes I write. For me, Pelit's fills the place of those cafés in Vienna. At one table the mustachioed British attaché is talking to Afitap Hanim, an assistant at the University, with a deep voice and lovely eyes. At another table a mezzo is busy trying to turn the head of an Italian tenor, a guest artist newly hired for the Opera. At another, Salih the bird-painter and his wife are talking, doubtless about painting. Over there are two male opera-singers, like a couple of old hags, deep in backstage gossip.

I did say, didn't I, that the air of this café is redolent not only of European cigar-tobacco and cheroots, but of culture.

Now Tuesday is the German au pairs' day off and it is they who fill the café. These girls, who work as nurse-maids or housekeepers for wealthy Istanbul families, avidly eat their Apfelkuchen and drink milky Nescafé. They laugh and talk. It gets so that the people from the Opera can't find any room and go away again. On that day of the week the café ceases to be the Café Bighead. On Tuesdays the atmosphere of Pelit's is laden with girls. They make their presence felt with all their vivacity, all their electricity.

Among them is a Brünnhilde straight out of Wagner, and she is the one I like best. Brünnhilde is from Graz. She speaks with a delightful Austrian accent. She has come to Istanbul just to see the country and get some experience. She teaches German and deportment to the twin daughters of a parvenu family. She originally did a doctorate at the University of Graz, on Rilke. Tall, blonde, letting half of her hair hang down by her left eye à la Veronica Lake; a lovely girl, sweet as a nut. Unlike our girls, she does not remove the hair on her legs with depilatories or razors; looking at them makes me think of other places where hair grows. I get randy. But does womanizing befit a man of culture? I play the satiated man of the world. To this end, to make my satiety look more natural, I satisfy my needs elsewhere, before Tuesday. This civilized – God forgive me! – satiety magnifies me even more in her eyes.

And there's Ingeborg. Ingeborg is from Upper Pomerania, a well-built girl, thick-necked. A girl who, with her full breasts and cheeks like polished apples, could stand as a monument to health. She's a lector at the Goethe Institute, at that time newly-founded. And there's Roxanne. Speaks German like a native. Even if her name should mislead you, it's obvious from her dark colouring that she's pure Turkish. Roxanne is the daughter of an old and well-to-do family, intelligent and with a thirst for culture. You couldn't call her beautiful but she is extremely well-groomed. She dresses smartly and with taste. She rides several days a week at the

Equestrian Club. The four of us make an agreeable group. We don't engage in idle chatter. We talk about culture, about literature, philosophy, art history, archaeology. We pretty much forget where we are. The topic of Wagner, suggested by association of ideas with Brünnhilde's name, has long since been exhausted, so now we reach many a platonic and intellectual orgasm by way of, for instance, Lehnau's *Weltschmerz*, Nietzche's *Ecce Homo*, Heine's *Atta Troll*, Kafka's *Letters to Milena*. And I, after all, am Assistant to the Professor of the History of Art, so sometimes I take them and walk them round the Süleymaniye, the Blue Mosque, the Kariye, the Topkapi Palace. Sometimes I take them up to Büyük Chamlija. While pointing out the skyline of mosques and palaces across the water, I take the opportunity of slipping in a comparison lifted from Dagobert Frey, one of whose articles I had translated. I do it dogmatically, as if I had invented it there and then. 'Look,' I say, 'at the astonishing harmony between Turkish architecture and nature. In Rome all the historic buildings grow out of the ground, side by side, like mushrooms. How harmoniously have the Turkish architects, on the other hand, put their mosques onto the rises and falls of the ground, taking into consideration the positions of the earlier Byzantine monuments, to create this miraculous skyline.'

Dear Brünnhilde throws back her hair like a foal's mane and constantly takes notes. Flashes of gratitude in Roxanne's eyes. She unquestionably has it in mind to retail all this to someone else.

Well, that's how my days passed in that period.

One Tuesday, Roxanne came to Pelit's with a beautiful girl. A girl no one here had ever seen or come across. She had dimpled cheeks, dimpled knees, dimpled ankles. She had quite certainly got dimples in the small of her back and on her buttocks. Taller than average, her anthracite-black hair gleaming, the nails of her fingers and toes painted carmine, her white skin bright, her eyes bright; a sparking creature. Wouldn't you know it; they went and sat at another table. I didn't take my eyes off the new arrival. She had rather big hands, but I like women with big hands, provided they're smart. The way she smokes her cigarette is smart, the way she crosses her legs is smart.

Their air of playing truant from school and their excessive gaiety might even make one think there was some kind of lesbian relationship between her and Roxanne. The following Tuesday they came again together. I was sitting with Ingeborg and Brünnhilde. Roxanne came over to us and tersely introduced her companion: 'My friend Zuhal.'

Zuhal didn't look a particularly intellectual sort of girl. She listened to the conversation uninterestedly and sometimes concealed a yawn, mouth closed. She weighed me up quickly enough. She didn't go much on me. A mutual understanding was unlikely. That was perfectly clear. Obviously she didn't like Brünnhilde either. She quite took to Ingeborg; I don't know if it was because Ingeborg knew a certain amount of Turkish. She listened with a total lack of enthusiasm to what I had to say. She looked at me with an air of wonder verging on contempt and mockery, as if thinking, 'Ah yes, I've heard tell of such specimens.' I knew it, I could see it; she despised me. But might not her determination to make this lack of interest obvious, her insistence on drawing attention to it, be interpreted as some kind of symptom of interest? She kept fidgeting. She looked at her small wristwatch and said, 'Come on! I thought we were going to the folk-dancing at the Exhibition Palace?'

For a time she leafed through the magazines on the table. It was evident that she was bored at not understanding what we were talking about. Nor did she attempt to conceal this fact. After a while she stood up and went to the ladies' room. She had long legs and a slender waist. The way she stood, the way she walked; everything about her became her, and she was aware of it; a creature consummately at her ease.

Quietly I said to Roxanne, 'Who is she, love?'

No less quietly she replied, 'She's a kind of home-grown au pair. She nurses my grandmother. My mother's family take Grandma off every year to Bad Nauheim for a check-up. This counts as Zuhal's leave. I let her tag along with me. We get on very well. She never got beyond middle school but she's astonishingly intelligent. One of those people who have never learned anything but know everything. When I'm with her I never notice the time passing. I find her really entertaining.'

'Doesn't she read anything at all?'

'She really has it in for anyone who reads. She calls people who've had an education "You with the specs," disparagingly. Even if they don't wear specs. She has someone called Granny Sati, the midwife back in her village, who's been her mentor. She's trained her to be totally unpredictable. Sometimes she blurts out what she has to say and sometimes she surprises you by producing perfectly-formed sentences. She really is a crazy mixed-up kid.'

And now this crazy mixed-up kid is sitting facing me.

'Still, you row very well, dear,' she says.

The first time she has called me 'dear'.

A promising start to the evening.

I don't answer. What is there to say? Some remarks don't call for an answer.

Besides, to put aside false modesty, I do row well. My rowing is like poetry. It's the only thing in all the world that I do beautifully. I am fully aware of this.

What I prefer even to the music of Telemann and Bach is to give myself up to the pleasure of this rhythm for hours, all by myself, in Moda Bay, sometimes very early in the morning, sometimes at the loneliest hours of night.

Yes, in three weeks, that is to say since first we met, that has been her first show of favour towards me. This is the disagreeable girl who for three weeks, at our every meeting, has looked not at me but through me, as if I were transparent, and turned her eyes in some other direction, who has pursed her lips at my witticisms which make the other girls laugh, has wrinkled her nose at my remarks which the other girls listen to with interest; who, in short, has a very poor opinion of me. Should I now say, 'Thank you' to her, or 'You are too kind'? What would be the point?

One day in Pelit's, at noon, when no one much was about, I was at my table reading when I sensed near me the presence of a fragrant shadow. I looked up. It was her. She was almost close enough for her stomach to touch the edge of the table and, in that pose which suited Marilyn Monroe so well, she stood erect in front of me, her legs a little apart, as if issuing a challenge.

'Aren't I a mother's child too?'

'I don't understand.'

'Don't you reckon I'm a person?

In the tone of her voice there was just the faintest trace of the northeaster blowing across the Black Sea. Somewhere round Giresun.

'You talk an awful lot and you know an awful lot but you're jolly slow in the uptake. Consider me today as an au pair (she pronounced it *awe pair*) girl on holiday.'

'What's the idea?' I said. 'You don't like me.'

'True,' she replied. 'But I warmed a little towards you the other day. You know, when the cherry icecream got spilt on top of my white shoe and you immediately bent down and wiped it with your hankie. As you straightened up you were all red in the face. Where are we going to go?'

Her directness appealed to me. 'Wherever you want. Do you like walking?'

'As long as it's downhill'.

'Fine!'

We drove up to Chamlija. She bought some pumpkin-seeds from an itinerant nut-seller. She left a pebble on the saint's tomb. Then we walked to Küplüje, by a path little known even to people who have lived all their lives in Istanbul, never mind about people from Giresun. All the way, watching out for her middle-school complex, I committed no act of what she would call pedantry. To begin with, I said nothing except in reply to her questions. When she did ask a question, I gave factual, brief and down-to-earth answers. I think she warmed a bit more towards me.

She asked, as if she didn't know, as if she hadn't heard it from Roxanne, 'What work do you do, love?'

'I'm a writer.'

'Who do you write for?'

'People who read and go to the theatre.'

'What do you write?'

'Stories, plays.'

'Why do you write?'

'So that they should read it and approve, like it and applaud. What did Molière say? "The purpose of art is to be approved."' She seemed to be getting angry. I'd done it again; I'd let another alien name intrude.

'If they do approve, then what?'

'Then I'm happy. Everyone has some ray of comfort in this world. To leave something of oneself that will survive – do you find this absurd?'

'Very,' she said. 'Everybody is fully taken up with himself. Everybody has his own tale to tell, which is not like anybody's else's. Everybody is acting out a play he's written himself. He listens to yours with only half an ear. Then he forgets all about it. He dismisses it entirely from his mind.' She spat out a pumpkin-seed and added, 'And what you've written ends up at best as screws of paper for the chaps who sell pumpkin-seeds.'

'That may be,' I said.

'Only trees have the gift of surviving till tomorrow,' she said, pointing to a plane tree in front of us. 'I wonder what this grand old chap has seen. And what he will see. Seasons come and go, people are born and die. He still stands. He's still there, not giving a damn for anyone, not trying for approval or popularity.' She spat out another pumpkin-seed.

Being from Beylerbey myself, I'm very fond of this road. It brings back my childhood. The weather is very close and hazy. I am leaving all the talking to her.

'This writing business, does it at least bring in any money?'

'Not so's you'd notice.'

'In that case, you're living on your capital, like the rest of us.'

'You flatter me. I'm also a university teacher. To be more accurate, I'm an assistant. A professor's stooge. I translate the German professor's lectures for him.'

'What does he talk about, the German professor?'

'History of Art. How art has developed during the course of history.'

41

'So that the students can sell it to some other customer?'

We are pressing on along the pathway. 'I adore this place,' she says.

I had known this path for donkey's years; it so happened that my friend Tanpinar discovered it for himself just a few weeks ago. He said to me, 'That was the day I understood why Giorgione painted his Naked Venus lying beside Nature, seen through the open window and supine like her. Those rises and falls gave me the feeling of a living female entity.'

Tanpinar is a man of subtle spirit. Goodness knows what sublime inspirations he has drawn from which folds of the terrain. A different association of ideas has brought me to the same feeling. Whenever I look at the ridges above Chengel-köy, particularly in hazy weather like this, there is an area in the midst of those naked curves, a mound that calls to mind a woman's lower abdomen and in front of it the bushy darkness of a small, dense coppice.

If I start talking to Zuhal about Ahmet Hamdi Tanpinar, she may think it's pedantry.

If Ahmet Hamdi isn't taught in the syllabus of the middle school which she failed to finish in the appointed time, it may be that she's never heard of him. Still, I can't keep my mouth shut. I've just got to share my feelings with someone. 'A poet friend of mine,' I said, 'pointed out the resemblance between this place and Giorgione's Venus.'

'Is he a professor too?'

'No, he's a poet.'

'If he's a poet, why doesn't he say what he himself feels, instead of showing off his book-learning about Georgie or whoever it was?'

I defy you to explain to her that even richer pleasures may be obtained from nature if culture is brought in too. I keep quiet. Yet it may be that she's right. It may be that direct perception, without references or association of ideas or interpretation, can give one more unsophisticated, more virginal, more intense a pleasure. I don't say that either. There's never any harm in silence.

'And what other tripe do you teach in your lectures?'

'Painting, sculpture and all that. Who painted such-and-such a picture, when and why.'

'What's the use of that?' Something must have caught her eye; she's running, as joyously as a child. Gracefully she bends down. 'A four-leafed clover!' she cries. She picks it gently, so as not to crumple it. She caresses it, kisses it and holds it under my nose. 'Who done this, then?' she says. For some reason she exaggerates her local dialect when she's being witty. 'Can the Prof explain that?'

We walked on a bit further and suddenly she stopped. Her eyes were fixed on something ahead. 'Look at that oak,' she said. She pointed to a dignified oak standing alone and looking down on the Bosphorus from a hillock. 'That's a lot like my oak. It lived just like this one, on its own, apart from any other trees. You cannot imagine how much I loved it.'

She took off her shoes and pushed them into my hand, together with the screw of paper that held the pumpkin-seeds. She flew barefoot down the slope, straight to that oak, and hugged it very tight. When I reached her, her cheeks had grown pink. She sat down on the ground. No, that's not the word; she settled like a butterfly.

'I had an oak there,' she said. 'When I was twelve or thirteen I was really in love with it. If I was upset I would go and tell it what was troubling me. I used to press my chest and my cheek against its rough bark. I talked to it non-stop. It was silent and listened to me. And because it was silent it listened properly. People don't listen to people. They listen with half an ear. While they're listening to you they're thinking about what they're going to say next. But that tree used to listen. It had such a powerful look. It had acorns with hard skins. Its leaves were such a bright green.' She spoke as if talking in her sleep, her eyes on the oak. Suddenly she collected herself. She said, 'What nonsense I'm talking!' and lit a cigarette. 'Have I caught a dose of the show-offs from three visits to Pelit's, or what?'

Again she was lost in reverie. 'Sometimes I used to go and lie down with the soles of my feet pressed against it.' As if it had suddenly occurred to her, she pressed her soles against the trunk. 'It was as though something or other was passing from it into me. I'd shut my eyes and dream.'

I was listening to her as if I myself were an oak. What unheard-of dimensions sometimes exist in the most unlikely people. I felt as if I had discovered a new continent. I said, 'My dear, I've come to know you only today. I love your simplicity, your sincerity, your directness.'

She didn't utter a word. She was examining her nails, very intently.

'You don't need books or guides. You find all beautiful things for yourself and enjoy them as you please. And why? Because you are flawlessly beautiful. You are a part of beauty; it's easy for you to short-circuit with other examples of beauty.'

She liked it all. But she clearly thought my use of the term 'short-circuit' odd; equally clearly she knew it as the name of an electrical fault. 'Did that come out of a book too?' she said.

'No,' I replied. 'Straight from the heart. From myself. My dear, you perceive everything; can you not perceive that? You are an unalloyed product of nature. You are as vivid, alive, vital and bright as that leaf. You shine far brighter than other girls.'

In case she should think I was being flirtatious, I looked away from her and said, chewing a blade of grass I had plucked, 'You put it very well just now. How bright is the green of the leaf.'

Some words of Goethe occurred to me. Somewhere he says, 'All doctrine is more or less hazy. But how bright is the leaf of a tree.' That veteran virtuoso of life, does he ever miss the difference between abstract and concrete, thinking and living?

The habitués of Pelit's and their like, with their thirst for culture, their intelligent looks, their percipience, their discernment; I revere them all, because we are all aspirants in the same mystic order. We are all on the same wavelength. But this person with me is a force of a totally different kind. A force like nature, like clover, like grass, like flowers, like a tree, like a bough. She exists and she is there, as she said a moment ago of the plane tree.

As she sat, feather-light, she pulled herself together. 'Come on!' she said. 'That's enough chatter.'

The promotion from pedant to chatterer is a good sign.

First we went down to Beylerbey and from there we walked to Chengelköy. We ate at the restaurant next to the Chengelköy quay. She got them to bring Bombay duck, chops and fried aubergines. She eats daintily, holding her knife and fork elegantly, like a diplomat's wife. Between courses she lit a Pall Mall. I watch the way she holds the cigarette in her long fingers, her head slightly inclined to one side, and the way she exhales the smoke. The meal over, she suddenly looked at her watch. 'It's late. Pay the bill and let's go.'

On the way, she fell silent. I said, 'I've even started to call you dear. Won't you do the same for me?'

'I can't, not just like that. Give it time. Let it come from my heart.'

'You know best, dear. When shall we see each other again?'

'Can't say.' Then she gave a sudden smile. 'We'll scheme something up.' With her dimpled cheeks she was now ten times as lovely.

She came once more to Pelit's. Again she was bored and she yawned. Roxanne had said she could be foul-mouthed, but neither on the Küplüje outing nor at the table at Pelit's did she go beyond the bounds of good manners. Her pronunciation of Ingeborg's name, without the *r*, was simply because her tongue couldn't cope with that particular sound. If it were not so, would she have tried to euphemize the name of the Goethe Institute, where Ingeborg worked, into 'the Bum Institute'?

I don't know if it was something in the atmosphere of Pelit's or what it was, but when we were there she would at once become hostile to me. I noticed that when we happened to be alone there together she never missed a chance to put me down. On one such occasion she asked, 'Why the poses, the cheroots, the wry European-type smile, when you were sitting next to that uncouth girl?'

'You're right,' I said. 'But this is a universal law. The male always wants to win the female's approval. If he's a cockerel, he crows. If he's a bugler, he blows the bugle. If he's got a voice, he sings. If he's a swimmer, he dives from the high board. If he's rich, he spreads his wealth in front of her. The speciality of writers and artists and thinkers, or, as you would put it, the chaps with the specs, is verbal gymnastics, and there you are: pedantry!'

She graciously smiled. 'If you didn't go in for pedantry I would find you more attractive.'

Suddenly I counterattacked. 'Now don't get cross,' I said, 'but do you think you're totally free of affectation and pretentiousness? Why do you smoke those swanky Pall Mall? Why do you cross your legs like a fashion model? Why do you wear nail varnish? Why do you put on the European perfumes you learn about from Roxanne? Why do you have your hair set? Why the mascara on your long eye-lashes, which don't need it? Why the lipstick on your full red lips, which are more beautiful than lipstick?'

She seemed to be angry. The dimples on her mocking face disappeared. She was frowning. To recover her composure she again brought the ends of her hair to her nose and sniffed at them.

'Don't you try to challenge me!' she said. 'My smoking Pall Mall, my perfume, my nail varnish, my lipstick, my clothes; none of that is affectation. That's my Sunday-best outfit. It's what I wear when I go out among people. My name's a fake too, like a hair-piece or a wig. My real name's not Zuhal, it's Hamide. Surprised, aren't you? Isn't Zuhal more appropriate to that posh house I work in? If I want to, I can strip off all these accessories in an instant and toss them away. All that's necessary is that the man I'm with should be worth it. If not, one goes on with the play-acting. Capito?' (Now where had she got that word from?) 'But you chaps with the specs can't strip off so easily. If you didn't keep coming out with all the book talk, the culture twaddle, that Kafka or whatever his name is and all the sayings of that chap with a name like Bum, you might not have anything left to say at all. When I undress, I come out from underneath. When you undress, maybe a skeleton comes out, but there's no you there at all.'

Scarcely a week later, Roxanne invited me to her birthday party. The party was in the boat-house of their villa on the

Bosphorus. To create atmosphere, they had turned off the electric lights, lit church candles everywhere and hung on the walls some icons and a few non-figurative paintings. From some antique-dealer they had got hold of an old-time gramophone and a barrel-organ badly in need of tuning.

Those who came by themselves were given a little envelope containing a card folded in half. On it was written the name of your partner for the evening. I put mine in my pocket without looking at it.

Ten or a dozen guests were there and one or two foreign beatniks. The record-player was playing warming-up music, lots of Nat King Cole and Frank Sinatra.

The hosts were Roxanne, Zuhal, and Roxanne's brother Sinan.

Zuhal came over to me and said, 'Have a look and see who your partner is.'

I looked at the card and then I looked at her. 'There's trickery afoot,' I said.

She smiled and said, 'It's fate, that's all.'

The bits to be eaten with the drinks, as well as the main dishes, had been ordered by Roxanne from the Grand Club. There was eating and drinking. First of all they did some of those dances where everyone dashes round in circles, to a barrel-organ accompaniment. Then, as usual, came the Western dance music, starting with the slow sort. Soon it will be the turn of the medium-fast dances and the boogie-woogie. It's fully automatic, their record-player. What with the cigarette-smoke, visibility inside the boat-house was down to zero. Some of them were smoking pot.

I found Zuhal's big hand in mine. 'Come on,' she said, 'let's get out of here. The place has lost whatever charm it had. Soon it's going to get even stickier.'

We walked along the water's edge. It was a moonless night, intensely dark. We came to a spot where she removed her sandals, tucked up her skirt and plunged in. She drew to the shore an anchored rowing-boat. 'Hop in,' she said.

I took off my shoes and socks and rolled up my trousers. I went alongside the boat and got in. She was just about to do the same when she remembered. She went back and fetched her packet of cigarettes and lighter, which she had forgotten, a half-full bottle of whisky and some pistachio nuts.

Now we are in the rowing-boat. For the first time she feels some affection for me. She is granting me a privileged status. For the first time she is calling me dear. In spite of my pedantry, at least she has found something to approve of. She is praising my rowing. This may be the beginning of praise for other things. Encouraging moves, for someone seeking adventure.

'That's the first time you've called me dear,' I say.

'One can't make love properly without that,' she replies.

Then, leaving me no time for surprise, she commands, in a drowsy voice, 'Come!'

Her lips suck like leeches. Her warm breath has the scent of chewing-gum with the mint still fresh. The boat slows and stops. Now it rocks slightly, in the wave thrown up by a steamer passing the distance.

'Whoa there!' she is saying. 'What a hurry greedy-guts is in! There's no need to go crazy. Can't you make love the way you row?'

She shakes herself and recovers her composure. 'Pull to that little yacht,' she orders.

I start to ask what business we have on some stranger's yacht. 'Do as you're told,' she says. 'The yacht belongs to Roxanne's family. Her parents are in Frankfurt with the old lady. When the cat's away the mice do play. Is it really Roxanne's birthday today? Don't you believe it! Why did we fix the boat-house party for today?'

We board the yacht. She points to the mast-head and says, 'Put that light out.'

I remember the story of the firefly. When he says to his mate, 'Let's go to bed,' she says, 'Put your lamp out. I'm ashamed in the light.'

I tell her the story. She doesn't smile. All she says is, 'Show-off! You've just got to dig up a wisecrack from somewhere for every situation. Only humans go in for false modesty. Is a firefly ashamed of love? Dumb animals are more decent than us.'

48

'In that case, why did you tell me to put the light out?'

'Putting it out means this pitch is bagged. It's code, get it? You'll see, some other daft couple from the party are bound to think of this place.'

The yacht has a cabin with a divan on each of the long sides. She takes the cushions off and spreads them on the floor, her movements suggesting familiarity with this operation. Clearly she is not shy of the light, because she goes and switches on the little light in the toilet. And she gives me her orders. 'Strip off,' she says, 'but first the stuff in your head. The showing-off, the witticisms, the philosophical chatter. When I make love I don't like a crowd of useless onlookers. They get under my feet. They spoil my pleasure.'

At the party in the boat-house they have turned the volume of the record-player full on, like a disco. The dancing is obviously in full flood. A good thing we got out when we did.

She undresses in the dark. The cabin is suddenly full of her distinctive female scent. In her eyes there is the confidence that comes of not being ashamed of her body. She undoes her hair and lets it pour onto her shoulders. With her long fingers she brings the ends of it to her nose and sniffs at it. She does this often; it's almost become a tic, but it suits the hussy.

In the half-light I taste the full splendour of her body. Like Italian girls, she hasn't shaved her armpits. In the centre of each of her large breasts is a nipple erect and challenging. Between her legs is the dense darkness of the coppice on the Küplüje road.

I cannot restrain myself. She can say 'Whoa there!' again if she likes. We find ourselves on the cushions, stuck together like two magnets. There is no more you and I. We have become we, one intertwined entity.

In the overture to two bodies' knowledge of each other there are bound to be false notes. Again I missed my cue and misjudged the tempo. My hussy is really keen on folk-dancing. At that trying moment she makes a joke, in a drowsy voice. 'Come on lads, come on!' she murmurs, in exactly the tone of the fiddler as he stirs the dancers up to even greater activity.

But it doesn't end as she wants. At break-time she knocks

back half a tumbler of whisky. Irritably she lights a cigarette.

As for me, I've become talkative. Perhaps in part to excuse myself, I spill out in words the admiration I have for so long felt for her. Lines trip off my tongue, lines from Sheikh Ghalib, Fuzuli, Karajaoghlan.

'What an overcrowded fellow you are!' she shouts. Then she relents a little. 'It's hard to find you in this crowd. Get rid of those boring people. When you're making love you have to be only two people. Then . . . Stark naked. Stripped. But not just your outside, your skin; your heart and head too. Forget about respect, being liked, false modesty. Forget everything. What is your name? Even that you must forget. To touch the ceiling in this business, your feet have to be detached from the floor, you have to break away from the world.'

'You're right,' I say.

'Time will stop, everything will stop. You're going to stop being, that's what it means. You'll no longer be you. You'll merge with the one who's with you. Till you reach the ceiling. After some time you'll open your eyes and be born into the world again. You won't keep droning on the way you do now. You won't drag chatter into love-making.'

'All right, but afterwards?'

'What do you mean, afterwards?'

'Is talking prohibited afterwards too? Saying what comes from the heart? Thanking you?'

'This chap's really got a thing about conversation. Let the thanks and all that stay where they are. I'll tear your tongue out! Happiness is a song with no lyrics. To spoil things with words is idiotic. Do you chaps with the specs always make love in this half-witted way?'

'On the other hand, there are certain details which add romance to love-making.'

'Now you're starting up with the details. Tonight is going to be as *I* want it, chum. This card wasn't dealt to you for you to chuck it away. This night, in this place, *I* rule. *I* give the orders.'

'Yours to command,' I say. 'I shan't spoil the magic by talking.'

'Ah! That's better!' says she. 'It looks as if you may amount to something after all. If I didn't have some small hope, why did I bring you here?'

After this telling-off, the second time is better. I don't utter a sound, I don't speak; that's why. In addition, I have learned the chart of her body and the course she steers. First my lips on hers, then they must slip down to her armpits and her breasts. Then she will guide my head with her two hands and say, 'Lower.' And when she finds the time is right, 'Come! Now!'

What had she said? 'There's no hurry.' Everyone's turn will come. First, for a while, the stillness of the oak-tree. A little later and her nails are digging into my back. I assume this is the moment to shift from being a motionless oak to the tempo of slow rowing. I appear to have judged correctly. I can tell this from her stroking my back with both her large hands. I don't notice how long the gently-plashing rower goes on. There is a billowing beneath me. It must be the moment to speed up.

This time she's in no state to say 'Come on lads, come on!' She is growling and beginning to breathe noisily. Sometimes she slows her breathing and sometimes she quickens it. Sometimes she even stops it altogether. Then an odd plain-tive sound is added, something between the moan of a child and the mewing of a cat. At any moment she's going to beat a tattoo on my kidneys with her two hot heels. Raging, in a voice choked with saliva, languorous, hard to make out, she says, 'Now go mad.'

Her command is obeyed. There is no pillow to bite. She is gnawing the edge of the cushion. I seize her by the hair and kiss her face. She is moaning, 'Oh! Oh! Oh!'

Sophisticated Zuhal has gone, changed into Hamide, the girl from Giresun. Her mouth is half open. Her eyes are squinting. Then she rears up once more. My face, shoulders and neck are soaking with her wet kisses.

How long is the interval between reaching the ceiling and returning to the world? I have no idea. I have lost count of time. For a while she lies there, her eyes shut, motionless, silent. The cabin is full of the mingled odours of our sweat. Then she wakes. She lights a cigarette. Whisky, pistachios, loquacity. After a while, 'Come on! What are you waiting

51

for?' From being an oak to gently rowing, from there to the
the tempo of the young men in the round dance, then, after
taking the last bend, once again into a crazy mad finish. So,
in intermittent delirium, rearing up and subsiding, we came
to daybreak.

I was unconscious. She must be an earlier riser than I. I
feel her firm living arm round my neck, her cheek like fire on
my cheek. She is weeping silently.

A motor-vessel passes, far off. She rises and goes into the
bathroom. She washes herself facing me, seeing no need to
close the door. She even uses the toilet. Blue-blooded girls
turn their back artistically when washing after sex. She has
no such concern. As she has given herself totally, what is
there left to hide?

'You're really a very good man,' she says.

'In spite of being a pedant?'

'If only you realized that!'

'I do,' I said.

That night I had begun to learn.

That was the start of a kind of secret honeymoon. We became completely accustomed to one another. She smiled.
Happiness suited her better than ill-temper. The home-
coming of the old lady she looked after was delayed another
two weeks. She took to visiting me at my house. The first
time she saw my books she said, 'Have you read all these? A
person could go bonkers with this lot.'

She learned all there was to know about the house. She
would go into the kitchen and prepare Black Sea dishes that
were totally new to me. For example, a kind of custard pie
made with black pepper. For example, hot rice with cold
fresh anchovies, cut small. While making coffee she would
sing songs complete, would you believe it, with lyrics. We
never went out. We stayed very close to each other. And we
started to make plans. We were both going to give up our
jobs. If she had her way we would sell all the books too.
Getting married wasn't essential if I didn't want to; we would
live as we were. Still, some day we might. We would settle
somewhere a good way off. No, not on the Black Sea but the

Aegean or Mediterranean. We would keep chickens. We would grow tomatoes, parsley and cucumbers in our garden. She would work as a nurse in the local hospital. I'd find a job in a local secondary school, teaching German.

Then Roxanne's grandmother and the rest of the family returned from Frankfurt. They closed up their summer home and went back to Ankara. When Zuhal said, 'I'll stay here,' I didn't have the courage to say, 'Yes, don't go, stay with me.'

I was the one who spoiled everything. Perhaps living is better than knowing, but to blend living with knowing produces an amalgam not to be despised. Besides, I had already been living a certain sort of life before. The arrow had left the bow. It might go a bit off course but it was bound to end up at its destined target. She'd say this was a load of tripe, I know. She can say whatever she likes, now.

Again I am in a rowing-boat. But this time I am alone. Again the oars dip as softly as before, again they come out as quietly as before, letting fall a drop or two of water. The time is seven in the morning, the season is autumn. The weather is hazy. The first steamer down from the Islands appears in the distance.

Already the scents of winter are in the air. The oaks have long since shed their leaves. But next spring they will come back to the world again, bright green as before.

The boat glides like oil over the dirty waters off Kalamish. The rowlocks creak at every stroke. The pivots need lubricating.

Where is Roxanne? Where is Hamide? What has become of Brünnhilde and Ingeborg? I have no notion. The Tepebashi Theatre has burnt down. Pelit's is a dress shop now.

That six-month spell changed my attitude to the world and to myself. It even changed my destiny. It taught me to know myself. It added a lot to my persona – no, 'added' is quite wrong; it subtracted all the synthetic ballast belonging to the clown I had thought was my persona. It erased all the immature showman's and interior designer's varnish; it taught me to find the unadorned human being inside me and to approach nature, people, possessions, everything, with the same sincerity.

I gave up smoking cigars. I stopped going to the Café Bighead. I began to find it nonsensical to keep a diary, to make notes, to split hairs, to rush in search of observations. I abandoned myself to my real self. I lived one day at a time. Perhaps I could never again, at any stage of my life, live that unalloyed happiness, the intoxication that was like a song without words.

Habits are never totally eradicated from the depths of the soul. By slow degrees I forgot my good intentions. Back I went to books, to notes, to scribbling. Yet though so many years lie between, even today, when giving a lecture or writing or attending a meeting, when I forget, as I sometimes do, and look as though I am on the point of returning to my old ways, I seem to see two honey-coloured eyes gazing at me mockingly from far away. I collect myself. I pull myself together. I become natural. I become myself. That's how deep inside me she has got.

You may consider this story as being in a way a humble thank-offering to an authority on life and nature, a model of sincerity and honesty, from a pupil of hers who has not yet managed to stop making a hash of his life; I mean, who still can't break himself of the habit of scribbling. At least until the day I become a source of paper bags for some other girl who is fond of pumpkin-seeds.

Where is she, I wonder? Is she alive? What is she up to? I pray she will never read these lines. Because I know that if she does she'll be angry. Because it would have suited her better if this adventure had been passed over in silence and had not been put into words. But, as I said, habits are never totally eradicated from the depths of the soul. In one way or another they contrive to escape destruction. It's my fault. She is entitled to be angry and to say, 'He's as bad as ever he was.' She'd be right to swear horribly. Absolutely, un-questionably right. It is my doom anyway that she should always put me in the wrong. Just as nature does.

It Works Both Ways

There are more things in heaven and earth, Horatio,
Than are dreamt of in your philosophy.

Not without reason did our clever Shakespeare say this. In fact, he never says anything without reason. And what he says he says more concisely and neatly than anyone else. And a good thing too. Dip your hand in his store of maxims and you can find a formula for every occasion. Suppose you find some close friend acting like a know-all. The way to bring him to his senses without wounding him is to recite to him those words of Shakespeare, with a bit of theatrical exaggeration so as to soften the reproof by turning it into a joke. Your friend who presumes to lay down the law on the basis of his half-baked wisdom and his own powers of reasoning will at once tuck his tail between his legs and come to heel. Just as Horatio did when *he* heard that wise admonition from Hamlet. That is, of course, if he has enough crumbs of culture to stand in awe of Uncle Shakespeare. If he hasn't, Shakespeare will have no effect on him. Nor will Kant, or Sophocles. It means you're banging on a locked door. Wasting your breath. Anyway, who tells you to make friends of dolts?

My purpose in citing distinguished witnesses from the history of thought is to prove that in comparison with what we do not know and cannot explain with our reason, what we do know or, to put it more accurately, what we think we know, doesn't amount to an awful lot.

After this preamble I shall now tell you of something that happened. It really and truly happened. It happened to me, years ago. It happened exactly as I am now going to tell it.

I don't know it you've ever been to Tiflis. It is a clean, orderly, tidy city. It is surrounded by mountains and is full of orchards. Its climate is mild. The Georgian men wear caps the size of aerodromes. They love wine, fun, jokes, singing four-part choruses and, according to the Russians, dodging work. As for the Georgian women, think of jet-black hair, eyelashes, and eyebrows, on limpid white skin. Usually those brows meet, over a straight nose. Add to the cheeks a touch of natural rose colour in exactly the right proportion. On the upper lip, some fine, scarcely discernible quince-down. There you have your typical Georgian beauty. We watched the Georgian operas, which take their themes from local myths; we saw folk-dancing which involved perhaps the most agile movements in the world. We sampled their famous white wine. It goes down incredibly smoothly but afterwards it kicks you so hard that you have no time to be surprised. The Georgians adore making their guests from abroad knock back glass after glass, to cries of 'Za vashe zdorov'ye!' and getting them drunk at table. They then amuse themselves by watching the resulting spectacle. So there is an aspect of them that has never grown up. Having been given prior warning by my friend Simonov, the novelist, I was prepared for their trick and didn't fall for it. But there were two other writers there, one Australian and one Somali, who practically had to be scraped out from under the table where they lay sprawled, blind drunk.

We were on our way back from a congress of Third World writers in New Delhi. I was there because of a book of mine that has been translated into Georgian and published in Tiflis. At the end of dinner they gave me an envelope containing my royalties. What does one do with royalties in a foreign country from which they cannot be exported? One goes in for some impulse-buying. The watchmakers' shops in the hotel lobby had caught my eye. The Russians take a pride in their watchmaking industry, as in all their industry. Not just today, either; it's been like that for a very long time. The excellent Sergizov timekeepers, which were known as railway watches, were the pride of our grandfathers' waistcoat pockets. Now, it seems, the Sergizov is no longer made.

The Georgian poet Abatzavili took charge of me and we went down to one of the watchmakers' shops. After protracted and meticulous study, he picked out a wristwatch.

'Take this one,' he said. 'You won't find a better.' The watch was just an unostentatious watch. But what marvels lay inside that unostentatious watch! For one thing, he told me, it was automatic. Next, it had an alarm-bell. Next, it was absolutely waterproof. It had been tested and found to work with the same accuracy in the forty below of Siberia as in the hellish heat of the Equator. What more could one ask? I took off my old watch and put it into my pocket. Carefully they attached the new one to my wrist.

I went to bed as soon as I got to my room. Early in the morning, the telephone rang. Befuddled with sleep, I thought, as I reached for the receiver, 'Isn't civilization wonderful! In the small hours the telephones even have a subdued ring!' There wasn't a sound in the receiver. Only then did I notice my new watch, still ringing quietly on my wrist. I smiled. Evidently my Georgian friends, when they gave it to me, had set the alarm for six-thirty so that I shouldn't miss the plane. I did say, didn't I, that they were fond of jokes. I got up and went into the shower. Through force of habit I took the watch off and was putting it down on the edge of the washbasin when suddenly I stopped. My new watch is waterproof, you know. I put it back on my wrist. Just for the hell of it, I held it right under the shower. The noble thing did not flinch. As I was settling my hotel bill, the manager's eye fell on my watch and his look became most respectful. Clearly this watch was the Cartier or Rollex of those parts. Well, let me be brief. With my marvellous watch on my wrist and four bottles of Georgian wine in my string bag, I boarded the plane.

Why am I telling you all this? Because, this being the story of a watch, I am bound to give you a certain amount of information about that watch's *curriculum vitae*.

When I got home all my friends said, 'What you ate and drank you can keep for yourself, but tell us what you saw.' I told them. But, funnily enough, what they were really interested in was not what I had seen but what I had eaten and drunk. 'Their vodka slips down the throat like oil, doesn't it?' 'They say they've got lashings of caviar. Is that so? Did you bring back any of the red sort they get from the

Caspian?' 'If I were you I'd have brought back an Astrakhan kalpak too.' Naturally, at this point their eyes would be fixed on the new watch on my wrist. 'The watch is from there, I suppose?'

I would lower my eyelids in confirmation.

'Congratulations! Automatic, of course.'

I would blink twice in assent.

'And of course it's waterproof.'

I would draw in my chin and raise my eyebrows, to convey, 'How can there be any doubt?'

Their eyes were full of envy. Just to spite them, I would list its other marvels: reluctantly, in a blasé tone, making little of it. Sometimes, when I was going visiting, I would set the alarm for half an hour later and it would go off in the middle of the conversation. General astonishment. For those who stared at me dumbfounded, explanations, given apologetically, playing it down. I would take my leave as if I had been a punctual man all my life: 'Time's up. I've another engagement at six precisely.' Dropped jaws. Then a crisp and decisive exit, leaving behind me an aura of interest. What more could one want?

The fame of my watch soon spread. Those who had seen it told those who hadn't. Comparisons were being drawn between mine and a more marvellous watch which an industrialist had brought back from America for his son. The debate on the two watches became heated, reaching the status of ideological polemics. Concerned, as being the owner of one of the watches, to remain objective, while conceding that smarter and more elegant watches might be made in America and, even more, in Italy and France, I explained that in this matter the Russians attached importance not so much to appearance as to solidity. In fact that is so, isn't it? You only have to look at their buildings, their mercantile and naval vessels and their town planning. It's all rather ungainly. They almost seem to consider aesthetics as snobbery. Right, that would be the start of an abstract debate on style: is it the aesthetics of technology or the technology of aesthetics that is meaningful?

The watch indeed had a stubby, solid look. I don't know

how often I dropped it, but it didn't stop. Under such conditions, goodness knows how many times a fragile Paris watch would have been back to the repairer. My watch did not belie its testimonials. I would leap from the eighty degrees of the sauna into water at zero and it took no notice. I would take it out of boiling water and roll about in the snow and it didn't so much as catch cold. Once, on the jetty of the Kemer Holiday Village, a lady interested in watches took it and was examining it when she let it fall into the sea. The water was deep. I dived in but couldn't recover it. For two days it lay there under the water. On the third day, a young fellow who'd trained as a skin diver brought it up. It was ticking away merrily. People who don't have much to show off about will inevitably find something. I used to show off about my watch. I took particular pride in it because it was a reward acquired not with a windfall but by the work of my brain, in a foreign land.

As the days passed, we grew more accustomed to one another. The watch became part of me. From the moment I first fastened it round my wrist, my personality had undergone a change. The alarm had made me punctual, regular; a man of decision and principle. Thanks to the watch, I was breaking myself of the habit of wasting time. Even, would you believe it, my former mode of behaviour, which was about as calculated as falling off a roof, had quietly vanished, to be replaced by a concern for timing which permeated my every action. That was not all. Its solidity and the fact that it was waterproof had, you might say, given me a shot in the arm to counteract my innate timidity. Now I had become a more self-confident and venturesome sort of person. In short, we had become very much like each other, assimilated to each other. We had established a terrific harmony. I was satisfied with the watch, while the watch, I believe, had no complaint to make about me.

I suppose this went on for eighteen months or two years. One day my watch – no, it didn't stop but it began to mist over. My unshakeable confidence in it was so strong that I couldn't believe my eyes. My first thought was that my spectacles had misted over. Then I wiped the watch-glass with the sleeve of my shirt. 'It cannot be,' I murmured.

'What's up?' asked my wife.

'My watch,' I said. 'It's misted over.'

'That's not surprising. You've been treating it roughly and it's taken water.'

'That's impossible,' I said. 'You know as well as I do, this watch is waterproof.'

'Show me,' she said.

I raised my wrist to her eye-level. 'Where is it misted over?' she said.

The watch, as though offended by our conversation and wishing to prove she was being unjust, had suddenly lost all trace of mistiness.

'Must have been some temporary fault,' I said. 'It looked misty a moment ago.'

'Lately you've been letting yourself work too hard again,' said my wife. 'It would do you no harm to see the optician.'

'All right,' I said.

Instead of my watch getting a name for invalidishness, it looked as if I was assuming that state myself.

Next morning, the instant I awoke, the first thing I did was look at my watch. It was misted over again. Less so at lunch-time, and by evening not at all. My wife, who instantaneously detects when I am uneasy, from my electric potential, said, 'Misted up again?'

'My watch?' I said.

'No, your eyes,' she replied. 'Look. And they're bloodshot.' She gave me some drops and I put them in, just for her sake.

Next morning again it was misted over and very much so. Noon came; no improvement. My hope lay in the evening. Evening came; no improvement. I have a veteran Greek watchmaker in Beyoghlu. He occupies half the narrow courtyard at the entrance to a block of flats. His workshop has windows like a shop but it's so tiny that there's room in it only for him; the customers stand outside and talk from there.

'Haven't seen you for ages,' he said. He has such a bushy walrus moustache covering his upper lip that the words coming out of his mouth sound fuzzy, strained through the mass of hair.

'I haven't needed to visit you,' I said proudly. But as I said it, I felt shame at having forgotten that my reason for visiting him now was the watch I was so proud of. I took it off and handed it to him. 'It's misting up a bit,' I said.

'This is a Russian watch,' said he.

'Right first time!' I said. 'I marvel that you guessed.'

He did not react to the pleasantry. He took his loupe and fixed it in his left eye. He turned the watch every which way and began to examine it. Like the close kin of the patient who wants to give him a bit of comfort when he is worried by the serious expression on the doctor's face, I hastened to say, 'There's nothing wrong with the watch. Nothing wrong with the spring or the alarm. It's just getting a little misty, that's all.'

He heard but he wasn't impressed. He took some small forceps from the drawer, opened the cover and with a little screwdriver undid some tiny screws, which he carefully lined up in a row. He opened the inner case and extracted the spring. As he always does when concentrating, he kept tugging at his nose. After a while he pronounced his diagnosis: 'This watch has taken water.'

Would you believe it? At that very moment the watch's alarm rang, as if to deride the master craftsman's diagnosis.

'And what a screechy alarm it's got!' he said, a little peeved.

'Come off it!' I said. 'That watch is waterproof.'

'If it's waterproof, where does it say so?'

Having been parrying this question for the last two years, always with the same answer, I smiled and said, 'Would a Russian watch have "waterproof" written on it? If it had anything written on it it would be in Russian.'

He had inverted the watch-glass like a delicate leaf and put it down next to the outer case. Now, after contact with the air, two drops of water suddenly appeared in it. 'All right. So it's waterproof. So how did that water you see there get in? Did the Devil put it there? Or is it steam from the engine?'

'You cannot get anywhere if you start off biased,' I said.

'My dear fellow, with all due respect to your superior knowledge, this watch is waterproof. It has been tested in every
climate. The fact that it's waterproof is established beyond
question, because for two years now it has been exposed to
water: to rain, to the sea, and to natural hot baths, and it has
taken no notice. It fell in the sea at Kemer Holiday Village
and lay at the bottom for two days and nothing happened.
How would you explain that?'

He didn't look as if he intended to explain anything. He
called out to the janitor's son, 'Sakip, my boy, will you fetch
Vortik Efendi, the tailor in the Anatolia Arcade? Tell him I
want him; he'll come.'

Vortik Efendi had been to see his relatives in Erivan the
previous year and since his return had been universally
regarded as an expert on Russia. The belief that he also knew
Russian was probably based on his own testimony. Vortik
Efendi arrived with his pincushion on his lapel and wearing
his armbands. He looked over the top of his glasses, first at
the watchmaker and then at me. The watchmaker turned
over the inner and outer cases and laid them flat. Then he
asked, 'Now let's see. Is there any smidgen of anything on
there about being waterproof?'

Vortik the tailor studies first one case then the other. I
don't suppose he could make out anything that might provide a convincing answer. Nevertheless, with the air of a
specialist brought in for a consultation, he was pointing to a
spot on the underside of the inner case. 'It doesn't call for
reading,' he said. 'You see that sign there, like a fish? That
means it's waterproof.'

The thing he was pointing to looked more like an archer's
bow laid horizontal than a fish. But this was not the occasion
for an astrological debate on whether we were dealing with
Sagittarius or Pisces. The watchmaker thanked him and sent
him off. Then he turned to me and said quietly, through his
walrus moustache as usual, 'You saw that, didn't you? He
couldn't read it: he was making it up.' For the first time that
day I agreed that he was right. 'Leave the watch with me for
a day or two,' he said.

When I went to the shop two days later I was hoping that

he might have belatedly seen the light, have at last abandoned his obstinacy, shown the watch to someone who knew more about it than he did and accepted that it was waterproof. I was wrong.

'The spring was heavily rusted. I've cleaned off the rust and the moisture. Take it and I wish you well to use it. But don't put it in water any more.' Then, apparently just to be nasty, he underlined the message. 'Whatever the opposite of waterproof is, my friend, that's what this watch is.'

I took the watch and put in on.

Next morning as I was getting into the shower I remembered the watchmaker's warning. I felt nervous. 'What difference does it make?' I said to myself. 'I'll take it off.' But then, ashamed of myself and, I suppose, feeling shame also at my lack of faith in the watch, I did not take it off. I put my arm, the one with the watch, under the shower but I stretched it away from the stream of water as though I was giving a Hitler salute. The way I saw it, I was thereby protecting its honour without drawing attention to the fact that I was doing so.

Next evening, back from work, I was going for a swim when a sudden panic came over me. 'I know it's not necessary,' I told myself, 'but just to be on the safe side I'll take it off.' The odd thing is that I then noticed I had taken it off already, by an unconscious act of will, and put it in my pocket. Next morning in the shower I again took it off, just in case. From that day on I quietly returned to the habit of protecting my watch from water.

There came a morning for which the meteorology people had forecast lovely sunny weather but which was in fact damp and showery. I waited in the bus-queue in the rain for quite a time. I went to the Faculty and gave my lecture. When I came out I looked at the watch. It had stopped. I wondered if this was the reason for the lurking unease I had felt inside me all morning. I took the watch off. I dried it and breathed on it. Nothing doing. Look at the machinations of fate! My lion-hearted watch had been exposed for years to rain and storm, it had been in and out of hot and cold water, it had lain for two days and two nights on the bottom of the

sea. Was it conceivable that it could give up now, in the face
of two lousy little raindrops?

The watchmaker understood, the moment he saw me in
front of him. 'Stopped, has it?' he said. He was like one of
those doctors who feel a secret pride on hearing of the death
of a patient for whom they had thought there was no hope.
Fortunately, he hid his smile, otherwise our thirty-year
friendship might have disintegrated on the spot.

'It's stopped,' I said. 'It's stopped but it hasn't misted up.'

For form's sake he put his loupe in his left eye and once
more took off the cases and the glass. A great silence fell. Not
a sound was to be heard in the shop but the efficient working
of all the timepieces, great and small, that had been restored
to health. 'They're very finicky, these non-waterproof
watches,' he said.

Look at his choice of words! Just look! The man's trying to
drive me mad. 'Cut the cackle and tell me what's wrong with
it,' I said.

On what occasion was it that the late Ismet Pasha used the
expression my watchmaker then came up with? Very full of
himself, puffed up with pride as though he'd coined the
saying himself, he said, 'Even I cannot save it now.'

'Honestly,' I said, 'I've not had it in water since.'

He pretended he hadn't heard. 'It was obvious it wasn't
going to last much longer. The best thing you can do is chuck
it away and buy a new one. And don't bother about it being
waterproof. You're not a deep-sea diver. You're not a skin
diver. Don't go in for a chronometer. Are you a steward of
the Jockey Club? Buy a decent watch and put it on your
wrist.'

I took my watch and strapped it on. It was then that a
miracle occurred. It started to go. Joyfully I pushed it in
front of his eyes. 'I don't go much on your expert knowledge,' I said. 'What, pray, have you to say to this?'

Although it outraged his self-esteem, although he couldn't
believe his eyes, he was unable to conceal his suprise.
'Amazing!' he said. 'Let me have it.' He took the watch
off my wrist. He put his loupe on.

There are two classes of people who are never surprised:

master craftsmen and intellectual pundits. It is a point of honour with them not to be surprised. That means that my master craftsman, who passes himself off as a master crafts-man, is no master craftsman.

'Ah! There, you see? It's stopped again,' he said. His aspect, pitiful to behold a moment ago when he was sur-prised, was suddenly omniscient again. 'It does sometimes happen like this. They run for a minute or two, then stop.' So saying, he instantly removed the matter to the theoretical plane.

'Just give me that watch,' I said. 'Goodbye.' If the door had not been fixed open, then would have been the time to slam it. I came home and lo and behold the watch was still going. 'I see it all now,' I said to myself. 'It doesn't do to take it off. It goes perfectly well as long as it's on my wrist.' But my surmise was short-lived. After giving me a certain amount of hope with its stopping and starting, it stopped entirely, as if it would never go again. Nothing availed, neither putting it on and taking it off, nor warming it and breathing on it, nor shaking it from side to side. I could not resign myself, or rather my watch, to this doom.

Having abandoned hope of the professionals, I took it to our Rashid Baba. I was desperate for somebody who would make a liar of the master craftsman. Rashid Baba, formerly of the Parks Department, is an amateur watch enthusiast. He loves and cares about everyone in general and clocks and watches in particular. Whenever I see him, he never forgets to ask after the wall-clock I have at home. I told him the whole story in detail from start to finish, as though I were unburdening myself of my sins to a psychiatrist. He listened attentively, not without taking it in, unlike Niko the master craftsman. You know how blotting-paper soaks up ink. That's how he listened. Then he took the watch and opened it up. He turned it about and then said, in a very gentle voice, apologetically, 'Whoever said it was waterproof was lying. You can tell waterproof watches from the seal, because they lock. Besides, they have an inscription saying how many metres under water they can stand the pressure.'

Is it conceivable that the Georgians swindled me? Yes, it

could be. But in that case what on earth was that horizontal bow? 'All right,' I said. 'But if it isn't waterproof, how is it that for years now . . .' I broke off. A weariness had come over me and talking had suddenly become pointless.

I left Rashid Baba's house with my head bowed. The rain had stopped and a stiff breeze was ruffling the puddles. Slowly I walked to Mühürdar. The sun seemed about to emerge from behind the dark clouds, then thought better of it. I had the foolish delusion that if it came out the watch would start going.

My memory was busy with the past. Had they really told me it was waterproof? I couldn't simply have invented that boast, could I? When that party was breaking up, the one where heads were so thoroughly befuddled, in that throng of people in the hotel lobby, all about to go their several ways, when the qualities of the watch were being enumerated, did the term 'waterproof' occur or did it not? It must have done, because – there, now it came back to me – my interpreter, whose Turkish was not all that good, couldn't manage 'waterproof' and had said, 'It does not swallow water.' I had smiled and corrected him and he had blushed and apologized. An interpreter is not a free agent; he translates whatever is said to him. But the Georgian poet who had sung the praises of the watch, mightn't he have made up this story about its being waterproof? He might and he might not. Let's say he did. If so, like the watch swallowing water, both the interpreter and I could have swallowed this joke. All right, let's say it was a joke. Then how do you account for the watch's taking seriously this appellation of waterproof which had been conferred on it, albeit in jest, and living up to it for so many years? Or had the watch ganged up with them and deceived me by masquerading as waterproof? That could not be.

My wife, seeing me preoccupied and depressed, had with her usual precognition realized that I was on the point of losing my reason over the watch. 'Don't upset yourself,' she said. 'Next time you get a bit of money you can buy a new one here. I saw some in the watchmaker's opposite Jahit's Antiques. It seems the migrant workers bring them from abroad. Some of them have alarms and some are genuine waterproof.'

Would you believe it? She actually said 'genuine waterproof', as if to mock me. 'And,' she added, 'there was some talk of their being Russian. In a way it's all for the best, isn't it?'

Strewth!

Well, that's the story I promised to tell you. It all happened fifteen years ago, but it still keeps nagging at me. I used to feel there were some things in life that could not be solved by reason, commonsense, or scientific analysis, but I assumed they were all things that happened to other people. When such a thing happened to me I was flabbergasted.

You are never the same two days running. Sometimes you wake up in your bed with a mathematician's certitude. You have swept your brain clean of all the parasitic elements, the dreams, the imaginings and the fantasies that mislead one's powers of judgment. Sometimes it is quite the reverse: you rise from bed like a medium or a sleepwalker. You abandon yourself to the flow of imaginings, intuitions and subconscious impulses of obscure origin. You pitch about on the waves like a ship with a broken rudder, not submitting anything to the test of reason, not fastening the chain of cause and effect.

I have looked at that event with both kinds of spectacles, or I think I have. For, like it or not, emotions and feelings still percolate somehow into the rational approach, while a rational mode of explanation always percolates somehow into the emotional approach.

I have reviewed all the alternatives. As I see it, I can't say I haven't found a clue. I seem to have done; I am still undecided whether or not to commit it to writing. If I do, some may doubt my sanity. If I don't, I cannot reconcile it with my conscience as a writer. They'll say I've funked it yet again. It's death for a writer to get a name for funk. A writer is supposed to write. He's supposed to be outspoken and courageous. If asked whether being a writer means being convincing or being sincere, I would opt for being sincere.

Even at the price of being ridiculous.

I am taking a fresh look at the whole business. Once the experts had said their say, it was no longer possible to deny that my watch was not waterproof and never had been. If you ask me to explain how, in spite of this, exposed for years to water and cold it never went wrong, I attribute it to the high state of my morale at that time when I would brook no criticism of its waterproof status.

When my morale crumbled, so too did the morale of my watch. For so long as I totally believed that my watch was waterproof, an equally unshakeable confidence and morale were passing into it from me. When the watchmakers shook that confidence, the spell was broken and my watch was doomed.

This is where you say, 'All very well, but what relationship does your morale have with your watch-spring?'

I am one of those who believe in the existence of an electromagnetic current flowing from person to person and from people to plants and objects. Why do plants that are caressed develop more quickly? We had an athletics coach named Abrahams who used to say, 'When you go to bed, take off your underwear. All day long, fatigued radiations from you have been sinking into it and all night long it will return them to you and you won't be able to rest properly.'

Moreover, watches are not like underwear. Can watches be called totally inanimate? Somehow they do have an esoteric existence. From the watch to you and, rather more, from you to the watch, there is an intimate two-way flow of electric current.

This thought sparked in my head that day in the watchmaker's shop when the watch was stopping and going. It didn't like his hand but when it came back to my wrist it worked. Then I remembered my great-uncle's wristwatch, which stopped the day he died. Not a minute before and not a minute after. Please sift through your memories. You must have heard of similar incidents.

Even if they are only one in a thousand, if you add together everybody's one in a thousand, a not inconsiderable total will emerge, such that you cannot put all of them down to chance. Watches, which identify and integrate with their owners, which have a common destiny with them, may they not be counted as the first little pioneers of a scientific truth not yet hypothesized?

What I am saying is that this relationship between watch and man may in time be understood. I am saying that it may perhaps be established with waterproof – I beg your pardon – watertight certainty that watches have a morale which they get from human radiation.

Have I succeeded in making you understand, I wonder? If I haven't, forget it. The morale of people and of watches has to be preserved, whether or not it is transmitted by radiation. It all works both ways. Whatever you give to something or someone, this is what you receive.

Indeed, if we take a slightly bigger step, it is even possible to think like this: Would you deny that the love that comes to us from others is most often a reflection of the love flowing from us to them?

Ali Riza Efendi
The Weighbridge Clerk

[This story came out in 1951. With other leading Unionists (see the note on the first story), Talat Pasha and Enver Pasha fled to Berlin in November 1918, when it was clear that Germany and her allies had lost the First World War. Javit was their brilliant Minister of Finance. Tijanis, Melamis, and Nakshibendis are among the dervish orders which were suppressed in 1925 but many of which survive; they maintain a low profile and the authorities tend to turn a blind eye. The Antichrist, in popular Muslim belief, will appear on earth before the Last Judgment and will be defeated in battle by Jesus. The Evil Eye is still feared by many simple people, possessors of blue eyes being thought particularly dangerous in this respect.]

I t was the middle of the afternoon. Sitting around in the station buffet, chatting across from table to table, there were Ali Riza Efendi, the retired weighbridge clerk, Kasim the house agent, the man who ran the place, some postmen who had finished work, some tax officials and several other men. The topic was the young fellow from the railway station who had fallen out of a tree the day before and broken his arm.

'What the devil was he doing up there? What could he have been looking for on top of a pine tree?'

'Well, it's childishness, isn't it? He got what was coming to him. The blood that's doomed to flow will not stay in the vein, you know.'

'I heard he'd climbed up to have a look at the girl next door.'

'Oh come on! If only Nejati *were* that sort of kid! What I heard was he was shaking down pine nuts.'

The weighbridge clerk put in a question: 'What about the hospital, then? What did they say at the hospital?'

'It seems he's fractured his left arm. Last night the students plastered it, after a fashion. He said himself,

70

while he was being X-rayed, that they hadn't managed to set it. The bone just pops out, he says. But today the consultants are going to see him.'

The Sergeant-Major said, 'I hope the boy isn't left a cripple. What the hell can he do on the telegraph key with a lame arm?'

'If it's a fracture,' said the weighbridge clerk, 'don't worry. I'd thought it was something serious.' There was a certain disappointment in his tone.

The man who ran the buffet muttered 'God give me patience' and shook his head from side to side. Kasim the house agent, fiddling with his prayer beads, was giving the weighbridge clerk a dirty look that meant 'What kind of a man is this?'

The Sergeant-Major turned to me and said, 'The Evil Eye is a fact, sir. This is how I see it: hundreds of girls, Turkish and foreign, come to the railway station. And you know he's a handsome young man. It takes just one of them to look at him the wrong way and that's it. You can smile as much as you like. This sort of thing's tried and tested. Let me give you a bit of advice. If you're putting on your new suit, make sure you wear old shoes that day. If your wife is wearing a fancy frock, that day you must go round dressed like a tramp. Saying 'Mashallah!' once, to avert the Evil Eye, can prevent many an accident. I heard tell of a man who told his friends about a bad dream he'd had and none of them thought of saying "God between us and all harm!" A full four years he wandered the earth in poverty. Do you know that story?'

'You ought to be a preacher,' said Jemil the tax collector.

The postman with the glasses chimed in from the furthest table. 'If anyone's given him the Evil Eye, it's the weighbridge clerk.' Seeing that the weighbridge clerk paid no attention, he made a trumpet of his hands and shouted: 'The shopkeepers have had experience of your eye. They tell me that any of them who sees he's got you for his first customer in the morning puts his shutters back up.'

Still the weighbridge clerk hadn't heard. 'It's a good thing that he fell,' he said. It really looked as if he could not forgive Nejati for having got away with a mere fracture. 'A civil

71

servant. Wearing the State's uniform. Is it seemly for a man like that to go strolling around on the tops of pine trees?' He looked round him but, seeing no sign of approval from anyone, said no more. Suddenly one of those inexplicable silences fell, a silence punctuated by the ceaseless clicking of Kasim's beads.

Two women passed in front of us. The elderly one was telling the other about some straw-coloured silk fabric the Rosebud shop had got. They went down the subway and emerged on the opposite side.

The weighbridge clerk said, 'When I was serving in Mughla, there were nomad tribes there. They subsist exclusively on pine nuts. Pine nuts and grapes. There's nothing there more plentiful than pine trees. Countless pine trees, untold, illimitable. And they're not stunted like the ones here. Twenty-five to thirty metres high they are, sometimes higher. The youngest members of the tribe climb up them like orang-utans. They do the shaking, the others do the picking-up. When that tree's finished, there's no question of climbing down and then climbing up the next one. They've a rope in their hands, with a hook on it, and they just toss it at the next tree, hang on to the rope and let themselves go into space.'

'Like Tarzan, you might say.'

'Mind you, every year they lose twenty or thirty people this way. If the branch proves to be rotten, there's no hope for someone who falls thirty metres.'

The weighbridge clerk having started to tell tall stories, the tax men began to discuss sport. They were debating the national team that was to play next day against the Germans.

The grey-haired postman had sent for the bootblack and was having his canvas shoes dyed.

The weighbridge clerk put his glasses on and murmured, 'Ah well, thanks be for another day.' And stretching out his neck, as wrinkled as any old tortoise's, he immersed himself in the newspaper.

The policeman on duty and the carpenter who had just finished his military service were walking up and down the platform. As they passed us, the policeman said, 'You can't beat the cavalry.'

'That's true, but if you come across the wrong man . . . Very disagreeable he was, our captain. Grooming took a whole hour. Half an hour for one side of the animal, half an hour for the other side.'

They receded into the distance. The postman who was having his shoes dyed said, 'What's the news, Dad? Are the Chinese beginning to see reason?'

The weighbridge clerk had turned to page four and was reading the obituaries. 'Oh dear! – Hüseyn Hüsnü Bey has gone too!' A barely detectable flicker of pleasure had passed over his lips.

'You knew him?'

'We were from the same neighbourhood, but he got on like a house on fire. He rose to be Talat's chief yes-man.'

The Sergeant-Major, who had always been an avid reader of the serialized articles on recent history, said, 'I trust you have forgiven him. Has this nation ever seen a Grand Vizier like Talat Pasha?'

The house agent, not wanting to be left out of the discussion, said, 'It was Javit Bey who was really the terrific chap among that lot.' He then fell silent, with the air of one knowing many things but unwilling to speak of them.

Jemil the tax collector abandoned the national team for a moment, to put in his contribution: 'He came to a sticky end, and all for nothing.'

The other tax collector said, 'They reckon there wasn't a financial wizard like him in Europe. My father tells how Javit Bey was in Paris once and said to the French Minister of Finance, "Well now, we keep reading so-and-so in the papers. What's up with your country's finances? Why can't you manage to balance your budget?" They explain the position to him: "The situation is thus and so. Our best financial experts just can't cope with it," and so on and so forth. "Give me a piece of paper," says Javit. He divides the paper down the middle, income on the right, outgoings on the left, and he writes. For fifteen minutes, no more, exactly a quarter of an hour, he writes figures on the paper. "There you are," he says. "If you produce a budget on the lines I've indicated, you'll save France." The Ministers and the Under-

73

Secretaries look at the paper. As one lets it go, another grabs it. Congratulations, thanks, wild excitement. In short, that's the kind of man he was.'

Kasim the house agent pronounced his opinion: 'But what's the good? We never appreciated him.'

Because the weighbridge clerk was sitting near the tax collector who had been doing the talking, he had managed to hear fifty per cent of what was being said. 'A load of rubbish!' he said. 'Idle chatter! Instead of setting France to rights, he should have set Turkey to rights!' He turned to the tax collector. 'I've forgotten a sight more than you'll ever know. In Mughla province I've seen them wrenching the gold teeth out of the taxpayers' mouths. Seen it with my own eyes. Is that your high finance? Is that what's called exercising governmental authority?'

The policeman and the newly demobilized carpenter passed in front of us once more, still talking about the cavalry. 'A thousand thoroughbreds are arriving from America any time at all. A purchasing mission has gone there.'

'What will they do with the old ones?'

'All they can do now is give them to the artillery.'

Again they receded into the distance. 'You can believe me,' said the weighbridge clerk. 'Never mind about Enver Pasha, they told the same tales about Napoleon II. And how can you compare Enver with Napoleon II?'

'You seem very worked up,' I said.

'I am, and that's a fact. See here, young sir, I'm over ninety. I've no lustre left in my eyes or teeth in my head. I've holes in my shoes. If it rains I can't go out. I was taken ill not long ago. I could have died like a mangy dog, with no doctor and no medicine. Well, am I the sort of man to come to this? Serve the State for all those years, work, and at the end of your life find yourself with no pension. And who's to blame? That . . .' (he tried to find a swear-word) '. . . that Unionist gang. Do you think I don't know what I'm talking about? Our department had a pension fund. Then one fine day, when the Unionists did a bunk, they took all the gold with them. A matter of life and death, it was. Their life and their death. And if at some future date the weighbridge clerk was

74

going to be ruined, who cared?'

The postman with the glasses laughed and said, 'Why don't you tell the gentleman that you were a follower of Ali Kemal? This chap supported the Reconciliation Party; that's why they stopped his pension.'

The weighbridge clerk may not have heard, or he may have been pretending not to hear. He continued: 'But what happened after that? *They* didn't inherit the earth. Who did? They'll all go, every last one of them. The kings'll go and the millionaires. All the ones who think they're God Almighty. The ones with their noses in the air.'

The man who ran the buffet was stacking the empty lemonade-bottles into boxes. He muttered, 'You're the only one who'll survive. You've seen them all off and you're still in at the last round. Gloat if you like, but keep it to yourself.'

The postman with the glasses, in a sudden burst of energy, got up from his place, came over and bellowed into the old man's ear, 'The Unionists died but they died with honour. Think about it: their families are still getting pensions for their services to the country.'

The weighbridge clerk went livid with rage. 'Get out of here! Go on, clear off! Don't make me do something I ought not to do on this blessed day in Ramazan! Where was the honour? What honour?'

The stationmaster had just come into the garden in time for the last scene. 'Look here, you,' he said, 'I'm not telling you again. I shall report you for defaming illustrious Turks. Are you one of those Tijanis or what?'

The weighbridge clerk was ready for him. 'I'm a Melami and my father was a Nakshibendi. Go and give the police my kind regards. We've got democracy now. I can say what I like. I didn't vote Democrat for nothing.'

'Come off it! You voted for the Nation Party. Namik here can bear witness.'

'Me? Me? Watch your tongue! You throw mud at every-body! You're outrageous!'

'Outrageous, is it? You're the one who's outrageous! If you're like this at ninety, Lord knows what you were like when you were young. This man is dangerous.'

'Dangerous, is it? The real dangerous ones are the dirty buggers like you! You're not ashamed to drink fizzy fruit-drinks in public in the daytime during Ramazan! Who was it the other evening who said "I'm a Freemason"? There you are, you're a Freemason. Why deny it?'

The stationmaster was bursting his sides with laughing.

'You stupid old imbecile!' said the postman with the glasses. 'And where do you get that from? I shouldn't mind if he only had the wit to understand. Do you know what they mean by Freemason?'

'They mean people who stick their noses into other people's business, like you.'

At that moment the Maltepe train arrived, covering everything in smoke. It was festooned with passengers. Some got off and others got on. Yervant the draper passed in front of us with his waddling wife and their daughter who looked like Yvonne de Carlo. They had bathing-costumes in their hands.

The daughter really did look like Yvonne de Carlo. Her raven-black hair was still wet. It was plain to see that when she had come out of the sea she had put nothing on under her wrap.

The weighbridge clerk made an elaborate performance of taking out his watch. He undid the scrap of wool in which it was wrapped and pressed the catch. The lid clicked open. He closed it again, replaced the woollen wrapping and put it back in his pocket. He must have been checking it against the train.

'That's how it is,' he murmured. 'That's what they call destiny. Some it corrupts and some it brings to sorrow and some it brings to ruin. And some, like Nesimi the poet, it flays the hide off.'

'The things you know!'

The pigeons, startled by the noise of the train, had taken to the air a moment before. Now they were alighting on the platform in ones and twos.

'All things pass, my good sir, all things.'

'Except you, of course.' (Yet again he didn't hear.)

'Beauty flies off and riches melt away. As the poet says, a sweet voice and nothing more survives in yonder dome.'

The postman who was having his shoes done said, 'If

76

you've finished with the paper, let me have it and I'll do the crossword.'

'What's he saying?'

'He says if you've finished with the paper he'd like to do the crossword.'

'The paper's not mine, it belongs to the tailor. I'm taking it back to him now.'

'I've got the *Evening Mail*,' said the Sergeant-Major. 'Take it.' And he handed it to the postman.

The two tax men were a little way off, pen and paper in hand, looking for an inside-right. 'Just forget about Rejep. Rejep's a weed. He can never get one past Erol.'

'Can't he just! You've got to have a proper striker in the forward line. The moment someone manages to break out and Rejep takes the pass, there's the ball, in the net.'

'All right, if you're putting Lefter inside-left, what happens to Muzaffer?'

'I'll put him left-half.'

The stationmaster asked the postman with glasses, 'Any word of the Captain? How is he?'

'I hear the doctor said it was cirrhosis.'

'The doctor said what?'

The doctor's diagnosis was repeated very loudly for the benefit of the weighbridge clerk.

'That's bad. If that's the case, he won't recover.'

I said, 'I've read somewhere that they've found a new treatment. They can stop the disease for a time.'

He gave me a nasty look. He wanted cirrhosis to be a totally incurable disease. 'Don't be childish, young sir,' he said. 'If that were the case they would have cured Ataturk.'

The man who looked after the buffet could stand it no longer: 'What a bird of ill-omen you are! Do you want everyone to have something awful happen to him? I've never seen anybody with such a wicked heart. If you had your way, the whole world would drop dead. Give up this rotten attitude. The man whose time has come will go, that's for sure.'

'What are you getting angry about?' said the old weighbridge clerk. 'Have I said something wrong? Pray God he gets better. He's not going to leave me his money, you know.

I mean, is a person not supposed to ask?'

The spirit had suddenly gone out of him. Like all old people, as he grew sad he became more pathetic.

The postman who was doing the crossword said, 'Used for writing, three letters.'

'Pen.'

'Won't do. Ends in k.'

'Ink.'

'Ooh, clever! Thanks, Stationmaster!'

The six-twenty train was panting into the station. The tax collectors got up to go: 'Two teas, one lemonade and there was one coffee from yesterday.'

'The backgammon debt going to wait till the first of the month again?'

'That's it. Well, so long, gents.'

To judge by the look on their faces, they had high hopes of the team they had selected.

After the train had gone, the weighbridge clerk said to me, 'I'll be off too, young sir. It's getting near time to break my fast. And I've got to water the flowers.' He did not even acknowledge the existence of the others.

I gave him good night and he slowly rose to his feet. He pattered off, taking tiny steps and ceaselessly jerking his head from side to side. When he had gone, the stationmaster said to the man who ran the buffet, 'What did you want of the man? You really upset him, and there he was, fasting.'

'Leave it, Stationmaster, for goodness' sake. He gets on my wick sometimes, he really does. Do you believe he's fasting? What a crafty devil he is! What a godless bastard! If he were a Muslim he'd be capable of pity. Didn't you see how his eyes shone while he was reading the death notices in the paper? Why does he stroll around the mosque courtyards? To see funerals, that's why. Anyone would think the lives of the people who die are going to be added on to his. He's got a wicked heart and that's all there is to it. If he were to die I shouldn't be sorry.'

'True!' said Kasim the house agent. 'He's no better than an infidel.'

The postman with the glasses said, 'The shopkeepers have

had experience of him. They say that if he goes into a shop, business is slack till closing-time.'

The grey-haired postman had finished the crossword. He handed the paper to the Sergeant-Major. The Sergeant-Major had turned round and was looking at the road. A group of girls and boys arrived on bicycles and pulled up in front of the icecream man opposite. Two of the girls wore sleeveless dresses, while the third, not to put too fine a point on it, was in a slip. The boys were wearing check shirts in all the colours of the rainbow.

The man who ran the buffet went on: 'Not long ago he disappeared for a while. We thought he was dead and we were quite pleased. The fellow's got nine lives. He had pneumonia when he was ninety and got over it. No penicillin or anything, either. Made of clay, they say we are. But this bloke's not made of clay, he's made of concrete. He used to go to the local school with my granddad. He buried my granddad, he buried my father and you'll see; he'll carry me out too. And my children and my grandchildren. We'll all die and he'll still be alive. They talk about the Antichrist, don't they? Who knows; perhaps that's who he is. When life is finished and every creature is wiped off the face of the earth, this is the chap who'll blow the Last Trump.'

The young people finished their ices and went off in convoy, larking about and laughing. The bootblack who had been dyeing the postman's canvas shoes collected up his tackle and left.

The seven-three down train arrived, and the seven-thirteen up train. People slowly got to their feet and went their various ways. I thought I would look in at the chemist's on my way home. When I got there, the weighbridge clerk was standing by the door, pitilessly interrogating the daughter of the Captain who had cirrhosis.

Morning By The Sea

Before anyone is stirring, the surface of the sea looks empty. One can make out a nocturnal heron or a couple of early-rising gulls in the half-light. They glide here and there, aimless and indecisive. There is a sudden pause in the busy fluttering of wings and they settle on the water. They put me in mind of a lot of dead-loss reserves who have come out to warm up before a football match. The real match begins much later.

A pelican, with its huge body and great wings, is patrolling high above. In the distance the put-put of a small motor vessel. On the shore, a tern pecking up insects. A mangy dog scrabbling through the rubbish. At this hour the land-birds are still befuddled with sleep. The plane tree beside the café is where the crows perch at night; it is said to date from Byzantine times. The swallows tend rather to lodge on the chimneys and cornices of the blocks of flats along the shore. Among the land forces, the early risers are the sparrows. They are on the balcony, picking at the bread I cut up for them last night. The pelican has come down like a glider, onto the water. He's looking round him.

These first hours of the morning are when I am king. Even though it may last only forty or fifty minutes, I slowly savour every moment of my reign. If you have this kind of addiction, you have to leap out of bed at five, summer and winter, so as to seize the morning before anyone else. But there's somebody who snatches from me the boast of being the earliest riser in the neighbourhood: Riza Efendi from the café. It is his pride that never in his whole life has he let the sun rise before him. I would not contest his claim.

At this hour, the personality of the sea is something else. The smells are different, the colours are different and, most of all, the sounds are completely different. The smells have a freshness, a freedom from wear and tear, a quality of not having been smelt before, of surrendering their scent first to you. The colours, admittedly, are as yet pale, dim and indistinct, but don't a lot of people prefer pastel shades because they give you the creative power to complete the shapes with your imagination? But the sounds! It is the sounds that are really staggering. The sounds in the first hours of morning are like the sounds first perceived by the first man in the first days of humankind. Totally new, totally fresh, spine-chilling and enthralling.

The receding put-put of the motor vessel, the beating of the wings of the white pelican as it lifts into the air with its beak the fish which it has startled by striking the water with its feet; far off, the first cock-crow. All of it matt, muted, pastel, real. Take the stick and beat the drum and in the first hours of morning the sound comes out quite different. Because the damp has slackened the skin? Not at all. It is because the diaphragm of your ear has not yet lost its virginity to the coarse noises of the day.

Now the day is gleaming.

One ought to spare the silence of the first hours of morning even the contamination of music. One should be quiet. Just be quiet and listen. All that the silence of the morning hours is for is to drink in and to absorb.

An excited flock of oyster-catchers have passed in the direction of Moda, frantically beating their black-edged wings as though late for an appointment.

Two beeps of a motor-horn have stabbed the stillness in two places. The driver of the minibus which comes to collect the primary-school children doesn't like being kept waiting. The little darlings who know this have been left on the pavement by their mothers before his arrival, their satchels on their backs and their lunch-boxes in their hands. The one they're waiting for, who's not yet in sight, is the podgy grandson of the local chemist. It's the same thing every morning. He can't get his act together; he just can't help it. Now he's going to suffer in the bus at the hands of the punctual ones. Enjoying one's superiority starts at that age, perhaps even earlier.

In ones and twos, the gulls are assembling. The vital match will shortly begin on top of the sea, the two sides being the aerial community and the underwater crew. Now some of

81

the birds that the locals call mickies have dived into the midst of them too. A bit further out, four cormorants are diverting themselves, plunging and emerging. Sudden uproar. The gulls, harshly screaming, are snatching fish from each other's mouths. There are crows watching this show from the top of the plane tree, from the branches of the oleander and from the telephone wires, with an air of conscious superiority. Why do I say that? Because there is an air of conscious superiority whenever one looks down from above. Besides, you oughtn't to find it strange that crows have an air of conscious superiority. Scientific tests have long ago proved that crows are more intelligent than horses.

At this precise moment a helicopter has just passed overhead. It will be taking the official dispatches to the Presidential palace at Florya. In spite of its deep clatter, appropriate to its highly important duty, our lot are so engrossed in the merciless struggle to fill their crops that they haven't even noticed this peculiar huge bird, its wings windmilling just above their heads. A heron or two, strangers in these parts, were disturbed and on the point of taking off, but seeing that the local notables paid no attention they have come back. The local notables are used to the helicopter. They know that its field of existence is separate from theirs. It is a huge bird on another wavelength, pursuing other ploys. Whatever its business may be, it can get on with it. It can save the country if it wants to. What is important at this instant is to still the clamour of their stomachs. Never mind the helicopter, they wouldn't care if an entire fleet of bombers were to fly over them.

Once this noisy breakfast episode is done and the gulls are restored to humour, they feel like a game. Musical rocks, we might call it. We have three rocks, one a good way out, the other two well inshore of it, side by side in shallow water. On top of each of them there is room for just one gull. For some reason the rock most hotly contested is the offshore one. All three appear and disappear with the ebb and flow of the tide. A gull will rush to bag that offshore rock and get on top of it. They all chase after him towards the rock. A contest starts, to the accompaniment of shrieks and screams. The rock

belongs to the one who first grabs it. Until he does so, it is
within the rules to obstruct him, to peck him, to push him
and bring him down. But once he's got on top of the rock he
can't be touched. Did you think the rule of first come first
served was valid only in human societies? The rule is also
applied in this game that the seagulls play. As far as I know,
no gull ever breaks the rule. None molests the gull who is
lording it on that rock. Perhaps annoyed at being pipped at
the post, perhaps bewildered and upset – never having been a
bird I can't say – perhaps with the anger of unfulfilled desire,
they start patrolling above him with all the power of their
wings. These gulls I am speaking of are the ambitious ones
who play all or nothing. Their goal is that best rock. Once
they have secured it, and only then, will they move off to
alight on the other two rocks, the second-class ones on the
shore. But the unambitious gulls, the sagacious and dignified
gulls, have perceived in the first scramble that the best rock
cannot be theirs; in order that the other two at least should
not elude them, they have quietly gone and tucked themselves in on them. When those who turn away thwarted from
the scramble for the best rock make for the other rocks, they
find they are too late there as well. Then it is a matter of
making constant circuits round all three rocks. The idea is
that one gull may get fed up, may have had enough, and take
to the air. And, they think, when he decides to do that I'll be
the one who leaps in.

I cannot imagine the nature or the source of the pleasure of
getting on top of that rock. To some extent I can understand
it in summer, but I just can't work out what fun there can be
in exposing your back to the freezing northwester, when out
there the wind is whipping up the sleet and whistling along
the shore, especially as the water is warmer than the land.
But it clearly must have some desirable aspect. The pleasure
of bagging that place is limitless. They turn hither and yon,
they stroke their backs and tails with their beaks, they puff
out their chests and swagger. Perhaps they like the sensation
of simultaneously standing stock-still and going to meet the
flowing waters. Perhaps they are simply enjoying the pride of
being in a spot that others covet. As I say, I can't imagine;

I've never been a bird.

Land birds cannot alight on the sea; that I understand. But why don't they alight on the rocks? Why are these rocks monopolized by the gulls, rarely the cormorants and herons? Why does it never occur to a crow, champion that he is in the intelligence tests, or to a swallow, to see what fun that place can be? Is this principle the relic of some treaty, arrived at after some pitched battle? Or is it simply a gentleman's agreement? You will say that the sea belongs to the maritime birds, just as the land belongs to the terrestrial birds. Very well; in that case, what right do the gulls, the mickies and the oyster-catchers have on the telephone wires? Why don't the swallows and the devout, mosque-haunting pigeons take exception to this? Why don't they stand up against this impertinent encroachment?

The sun has finally put in an appearance. From the table where I sit, the shore is invisible. So is the slope that has been turned into a rubbish-tip. So is the coast road that passes in front of the villa. There used to be an old villa which stood with its feet in the water; it belonged to Veliyüddin Pasha, the Intendant-General of Baghdad. They pulled it down and drove the new coast road between the great reception-room and the main body of the house. Remnants of the summer-house survive on the seaward side of the coast road, but from where I sit even they are invisible. Nothing is visible but the sea. And this sea, in the mist of morning, seems like a vast boundless ocean. With the rising of the sun, the shores rapidly take their place within the seascape. Yassiada, Kinali, Burgaz and the other islands, as though by mutual agreement, by some magic, some miracle, appear to rise instantly in unison out of the water, and by doing so they put an end to the Sea of Marmara's attempt to masquerade as an ocean. In the background the Straw Mountains display their silhouette. Sometimes, when the south-west winds of autumn are blowing, even Mount Olympus rears its snow-capped head, far behind.

The schoolgirls have begun to make their way towards their High School, which is at the end of our street, chirrup-ing as they go. And Lord! what a lot they have to tell each

other at this early hour of the morning! They talk in-
cessantly. Mostly, I suppose, they complain of their homes
and their parents. Maybe they are giving voice to all manner
of grievances, real or imagined. There is one in front, going
by herself at the quick march, never smiling, spectacled and
pimply. Further back there is another, short, with thick legs,
who rests her satchel on the tumbledown wall of the
summerhouse as she puts the finishing touches to her home-
work. These are of the breed that is going to produce
tomorrow's defenders of women's rights, the bright lawyers,
teachers and judges. How the calf will turn out is clear in its
infancy. The rest of them are of the kind who are set on
winning their School Leaving Certificates, for no specific
purpose but just so as not to be behind the others, and who,
once they've made some sort of marriage, will drop everything. All right, perhaps I am doing them an injustice; let's
say they're making an investment which will pay dividends:
they'll be able to find a job and taunt their husbands with
'You see? I earn my living too!'

Next comes a great loutish schoolboy in a hurry, with,
would you believe it, a sickly, squat, stunted girl. They
always go to school together and come back together. Does
friendship have any regard for conformity of stature? Then
there's another tiny girl, but already the electricity in her is
different from that of the others; a hussy. Four or five boys
trail after her every morning like tom cats. They pass cheeky
remarks and she gives as good as she gets. Sometimes she
smiles and they grin. Sometimes she turns round and tells
them off at the top of her voice and routs them. These little
girls really are something else. How well they manage to look
like innocent babes in winter, in their white-collared school
uniforms. But when summer comes and they put on their
tight sweaters and jeans, they assume the look of having
suddenly aged ten years, the attitude of little women. This is
an inborn gift they have.

The sun has thoroughly illuminated the opposite shore. In
the order in which they appear from our side, Topkapi
Palace, St Irene, the Süleymaniye, St Sophia, Beyazit and,
on the front left, more elegant than them all, Sultan Ahmet,

have begun to take on that slanting sidelighting beloved of the film-makers. This light brings out to the full their contours and details. The architects seem to have created these works solely for this light; in the sun of noonday and afternoon most of the details are lost. Master Anthemius of Tralles! Isidore of Miletus! Great Sinan! Mehmet Agha who wrought in mother-of-pearl! I lovingly kiss all your precious skulls and blessed hands, now gone to dust and one with nature.

Sometimes on an autumn morning, when the weather clears and closes in again, the huge black clouds passing in front of the sun begin a marvellous spectacle of light. In this gliding, which in cinema parlance we call a tracking-shot, they light up one of the monuments I have named and leave the rest in gloom. Then they glide away from it and move on to its neighbour, in gloom a moment before, and accentuate that. A celestial tracking-shot, this is, which leaves each in turn briefly bathed in divine light, making no distinction between Byzantine and Ottoman. This interplay of images, which has to be seen to be believed, is exclusive to the early hours of morning. And these images have to be assimilated and absorbed while they are present before us, because one day it will be too late. I know it, I perceive it clearly, I predict it. These pleasures have not been given to mankind in perpetuity.

Never mind that I am speaking with no sort of continuity, that I talk randomly, now of summer, now of winter, that I jump about all over the place. Grant me my freedom, in my forty or fifty minutes of kingship every morning, to turn time upside down, to pay no heed to the seasons, while talking of one thing to switch to another. Even if you don't, I shall do as I please anyway.

The shelter of the plane tree covers the café, the beer-shop attached to the tree, and the top of the ruined summerhouse. In these ruins a watermelon stall is put out in summer and on the Festival of Sacrifice this is where the sacrifices are made. On non-festal days, this is the park belonging to the scraps who don't go to school; as the educationists say, the under-sevens. By night it serves for lovers' meetings. But the lovers make no distinction between night and day; because they have nowhere to go they sometimes use this place in the morning hours too. They hold hands and are silent together, facing the sea. I have no criticism of that. There are two people down there at the moment, a tiny neat little girl and a very tall skinny thin-legged boy. Goodness knows what they're talking about. It is certain that they find society putrid; not to do so at their age would be reprehensible. When you're that age, the blood flows fast in the veins. The girl is talking too, to keep her end up. What they are discussing I cannot begin to guess. It's a good thing God has given mankind a throat, with which they have transformed the things in their heads into sound and syllable, and have made languages. Thousands of millions of people, everywhere, every blessed day, are ceaselessly talking in hundreds of languages, from Hottentot to Esperanto. They talk at home, they talk in the street, they talk on aeroplanes, they talk on ships, they talk in the city, they talk in the country, they talk on the radio, on television, in legislative assemblies, at diplomatic receptions, at the United Nations, at summit meetings. They talk to cajole, they talk to swindle, they talk to flatter. They talk to make witticisms, they talk to show off, they talk to accuse, they talk to assert themselves, they talk to relieve their feelings, they talk to prove, they talk to cheat, they talk to pretend to be cheated, they talk, my God how they talk!

Now these two small creatures are as yet only in the first stage of love, in front of the rose-coloured blank pages of first acquaintance. They are making the first moves towards fooling each other. Both are busy decking out for each other, in a well-devised wrapping of insouciance, the Sunday-best aspects, faces and attitudes which they themselves most like, which, when facing the mirror, they think suit them best. The girl, dreamy-eyed, is aimlessly drawing something or other on the beach with the stick she has in her hand. The boy has moved two paces away. He has seen a pebble on the beach; he positions it with his foot and takes a shot at goal towards the railings. At this stage the male is the first violin. The female is for the most part compliant and does not assert herself. The first trap she sets is to convey the impression that they complement each other. Both parties dress each other in the special qualities of their dreams, in accordance with their desires. I am fully aware of this, because I am looking down from the third floor. I have seen life and I have a coign of vantage. We always dress people up in one disguise or another, as suits our purpose. These rose-coloured days will pass away. Then comes getting used to each other, getting to know each other, having one's fill of each other and growing fed up with each other. Rough, selfish reality suddenly emerges from beneath those disguises. Will you then try to endear yourselves to each other, children, as you are doing now? If you can manage it, I shall be the first to cheer. Because that's the only way to handle this business. If you can't, you must cut it short and go your separate ways.

The boy has come over to the girl and is stroking her hair. In the chill of the morning, a shaggy dog has turned up; it must have broken loose. Now it has sniffed at the girl and gone. The girl has squeezed close to the boy. Neat little thing. Can't be much over fifteen. Even at eleven, girls tend to be expert at squeezing close. Even from the moment they're born.

The municipal dustcarts visit this shore once a week. The janitor of the next block of flats has put the rubbish into plastic bags and tossed them down the slope. The slope is our local rubbish-dump anyway. The janitor knows the boy; he has smiled and winked at him. The girl is new to this sort of thing, otherwise the dog wouldn't have sniffed at her. It's clear that the boy has made this place his bachelor flat for purposes of his platonic love affairs. What else can he do? He's poor, he has no home to take them to. When the relationship has developed a bit he may take them to the cinema or the disco, and from there to a friend's basement room. With the artifices of kissing, cuddling, and coupling which they see on the films, he will strive to prove his expertise and she her alleged innocence and inexperience. What a world! We cannot be natural even when making love. Everything about us is an act.

The first ferry from the island is coming, with the sun's rays on its right side. Audible from here are the rushing sound as it cleaves the sea, the noise of its engine, even the ringing of the engine-room telegraph.

The café-proprietor's swallow has changed boughs. A huge crow has uttered a loud bass caw. The power struggle over the rocks continues. As yet the status quo has not been disturbed, but there is a barely discernible activity on the part of those unambitious and prudent gulls who settle quietly on the second and third rocks. If they were content with their situation, you know, it wouldn't be so. But now their eyes also are on the best rock. Ambition has seized them too. Seeing the present occupier stir a little, they are immediately ready for take-off, in order to grab his place, considering themselves his natural heirs. But the instant that the lucky gull, having had his fun, flutters once or twice and becomes airborne, one of the vagabond gulls that chances to be taking a turn above him has assessed the opportunity. Down he comes like a dive-bomber and lands on the rock. Meanwhile, however, the gulls on the two lesser rocks have taken off for there at full throttle. Seeing the best rock occupied by the vagabond gull, they decide to fly straight back to their old rocks, but in the meantime two new gulls have come and perched on them. One should learn to be contented with what one has. Are the players in this game always the same gulls or are there changes of team? I don't know; I can't begin to guess, never having been a gull. But there's one thing I do know and that is that I have not seen the rules change. Nor do I think they will. Do long-distance birds, migrating birds, play this party-game too? I don't know that either.

I haven't spoken to you at all of the hidden rock, have I? It's just as the name implies. It's called that because it hides itself. The hidden rock is a very furtive rock. It is a lurking underwater projection, further out than the most sought-after rock. It never appears to view or makes its existence obvious, even at low tide, but it has its definite place on the mariners' charts. The masters of steamers and motor vessels gave it a wide berth and the local boatmen keep a lookout so as not to run against it. There's no mark or light on top of it.

One has to admit that man is a base creature, delighting in other people's calamities. Were it not for this characteristic, would Greek tragedy ever have come into being? What is Greek tragedy? What happens in Greek tragedy? If you believe what the books say, the spectator identifies with the hero. He is as full of emotion, revulsion and horror as if the calamities befalling the hero have befallen himself. In his seat in the stalls he has purged himself of these passions. Rubbish! I reckon that the truth is being concealed. It would be more accurate if they put it like this: Man is a scoundrel who feigns pity for the calamities that befall other people but inwardly rejoices that the calamity has passed him by. What does Lucretius say? *Suave mari magno turbantibus aequora ventis* . . . How sweet to watch, from a tranquil harbour, seafarers drowning in the raging billows! That, my friends, is the truth of the matter. That is the essence of tragedy. The rest is twaddle. It's a matter of buttering up the spectator by asserting his superiority.

That hidden projection, that stealthy rock; for how many luxurious motor cruisers, for how many million liras' worth of yachts it has spelled destruction, I myself witness from this very window. On one particular occasion when it split like a razor blade a speedboat doing a hundred miles an hour and hurled the pretty boy at the wheel ten feet in the air, I was delirious with joy. Another time, I shall never forget, there were two handsome young men, dressed in the latest yachting get-up like the yacht-club members in the TV serials, sunburnt, with wry smiles, pipes in mouths, together with three girls built like fashion-models, the Charlie's Angels type. They came swaggering over the sea one morning, complete with a pot-pourri of selections from the discos as background music, and with an almighty crash they ran aground on the hidden rock.

When the first shock of fright had passed – this is what always happens – they assumed they were going to be rescued immediately. The boys dived in and tried pushing the craft from side to side and from end to end. When that didn't work, they made the girls get out to lighten it. Because the surface of the lurking rock held one-third of the boat, there was room for only three people round the sides. One girl's foot slipped and she fell into the oily water. She came up talking to herself irritably. To begin with, they had supposed they would get over this unexpected adventure by making a joke of it, with witty dialogue as in – again – the TV films and would then resume their outing. But now the unbroken succession of mishaps seemed to have totally ruined the mood of these young ladies and gentlemen. Other parties must have been expecting them at Kalpazankaya or Yürükali or some such place. They were late. The confident, happy smiles of two hours ago had gone, to be replaced by damp hair sticking to foreheads, eyes enlarged with rage, heavy breathing and disagreeable faces. It was obvious that they were wearied more of bickering with each other than of trying to save the boat.

The girl I just mentioned was now sitting in the water-logged craft. She must have said something wrong, because one of the boys clambered onto the edge of the rock and boxed her ears. She found a flipper on the floor, hurled it at his face and began shouting at the top of her voice. Then she jumped into the sea in her shorts and blouse and started to swim for the shore, despite the other girls' efforts to stop her. She came ashore and clambered up through the thistles of the rubbish-tip slope. Twice as she did so she slipped and fell and was covered in mud. She emerged onto the road and, in her soaking shorts and blouse, jumped into the first car that came along and off she went, either home or to the house of some other man friend, just to get her revenge. The other girls must have been thoroughly upset by this incident. The bickering went on. The boys had thrown off their shirts and silk squares and were working in a muck sweat. All reserves of control were exhausted and all fuses had blown. It wasn't just their clothes that they shed that afternoon; it was also the poses of charm and civilization in which they had dressed themselves that morning. Another cruiser came by and one of the two remaining girls asked it for help. It approached; the owner was evidently making some suggestion to the young people. He came right up to their stern and, all of them helping, managed to detach the outboard motor. But even this did not serve to lighten the craft. The man said something and began drawing away. One of the girls jumped onto his boat. Our lot were very peeved at this turn of events but, preoccupied as they were with the fate of their half-million liras' worth of boat, were in no condition at that moment to make an issue of her unsporting behaviour. Once she had left, the last remaining girl really exerted herself. She was transformed into a model of the kind of self-sacrifice which does not leave friends in the lurch when things look black. With a small pan she was baling the water out of the boat, pausing only to go over the side now and then to hand the boys some implement they needed. And so they came to evening. The lovely day they had planned had fallen victim to the mischievousness of the hidden rock.

The engineer's hunting dog has just barked, for no apparent reason. He must have some justification in his own mind. Ah yes, of course; he's seen his master. The engineer brought him back from Denmark. Two hundred thousand liras they say he cost, a thoroughbred with a pedigree going back for generation upon generation. Fawning on the master is in his blood, a legacy from his ancestors. The engineer also has a thoroughbred parrot. It has learned from the television; it keeps saying 'Hallo' to everyone. Up to a point I can understand why hunting dogs fawn on their masters, and cats too, though cats are to some extent still capable of ingratitude. But somehow I cannot take kindly to the idea of a fawning parrot. You've got wings, sir! You're not earth-bound like those creatures; you're a bird, dammit! This is really rock bottom: at your lord and master's whim you quit that branch to settle on this one. Is it right to become court jester to a human being out of greed for an ornate cage and regular meals? To my mind, the parrot is the lowest member of the avian tribe.

Now the business people have started to come down the road, the ones with the briefcases. The janitor is washing the landlord's car. The engineer has walked over to his own car, looked up at his wife and waved. Is it because of their love for each other or for luck, as if to say, 'I hope things go well today, Mr Engineer'? His small son is also looking out of the window. Let his Daddy go to work and buy him nice food for din-dins and nice toys. That's right, sonny, isn't it? Ah, there go the couple, a husband and wife who work in the same office. They always go off to work together at this time, walking, summer and winter. They've made it a principle. They have a rapid but carefree walk. Both are square built and they are of the same height. They must be very indust-rious members of staff. Maybe they met when they were students in the Faculty of Business Administration. In a little while, Zülfikar Bey will come out, to take his grandchild, whom he coddles, for a ride in the car. One must keep up with the times; in every household the old folk too have to be given some function.

And now you see the chief advantage, which is at the same time the greatest drawback, of living on the third storey of the block of flats built on the site of the seaside villa of Veliyüddin Pasha, Intendant-General of Baghdad. Living on the third storey, one is deluded into believing that one can predict the future. The gull is going to fly up from this rock and its place will be taken not by the gull on the right but by the one on the left. If that motor vessel carries on like this it will run aground on the hidden rock. A day which begins well, and which there is no reason to suppose will not continue in the same way, will come to grief in this spot. When you look out from here, you know what methods of seduction that young man is going to employ, but you know also that in the end he is going to be trapped, seduced by that tiny neat little girl who looks as if she is being seduced. That businesslike couple; you know who is really going to benefit by their enthusiasm for work, and how so many lines baited with the standard desirable bonuses and promotions are going to be trailed under their noses, refrigerators and washing-machines and locally-produced Fiats, just so that they don't perceive what is happening but continue doubling to work every morning with the same zealousness. You who look down from here, can see it all, and smile.

Looking down from a height pushes a man into the conceit

of precognition, of prophesy, of empiricism based on observation. The third storey makes people into know-alls. When did I join the ranks? I conjecture what everyone is saying and concealing, their inward thoughts, their outward thoughts – all of it, all of it, like the back of my hand. It is always the same game that is being played. It may be musical rocks or musical hearts or musical perks or beggar-my-neighbour. Once you've grasped the workings of the games, and there is no game left that you don't know, the world becomes monotonous and life loses its savour. It has no interesting aspect left. I think this accounts for the antipathy one feels towards the attitude of 'I know', of 'No other way is conceivable', of 'I'm a shrewd judge of men', of 'I wasn't born yesterday'. Never mind about one's personal feelings; if only it made anybody happy. But it doesn't. On the contrary, one day it can make life as insipid as a tale whose end is already known. One must escape from the distortion that is the occupational disease of the third storey.

The ground floor is the floor of everyday street-level realities. The mobile grocery will be coming soon, and the housewives and servants of the neighbourhood are joining the queue. The place is full of the cries of street traders. Bargaining, haggling and, in the queue or from window to window, the gossip of the day begins. There is talk of devaluation, there are complaints of last night's television chat-show or a dreary series or high prices. Somebody says, 'Things could be a lot worse.' Somebody gives the Colonel's wife the good news that Orko's shop has got spaghetti. Someone else has found out where bottled gas is being sold on the black market, and passes the information on to the others. From the ground floor one does not see the shore nor the game the seagulls play nor the adventures of motor cruisers. The ground floor sees life and people from the level of all their shallowness and earthiness. It is full of small events and diminutive hopes. It is self-sufficient. Like wayfarers who get along a muddy road by leaping from stone to stone, it finds distractions for itself which, in the slough of low-level existence, will endure, will help to pass the time, will be talked about and laughed at and quarreled over and will end in reconciliations.

The block also has a roof-top terrace where the washing is hung out, a terrace which gives you an idea of the vastness of the universe. There is no view from it of the bay, the summerhouse, the shore, the road or the lower storeys. The only view is of the clouds and the open sea. There is a vapour trail in the sky. Sometimes you see the grey geese passing in a flock, like a V turned on its side, point forward. Then just the sky again and the clouds. Sometimes clouds, motionless as if nailed in place, sometimes clouds gliding terribly slowly, white or dark, lazy clouds.

The sky, the clouds and the open sea can be a world of tranquillity given only to those who have attained perfection, a universe of nirvana. Not suitable for run-of-the-mill mortals.

But the other day I felt curiosity. I went right to the bottom, descending that steep slope with great difficulty, until I arrived on the beach. The sea was softly caressing the shore as if it would presently lull it to sleep. Again the tide was out. There were two mongrels there, who must have been vastly surprised that the beach had all at once become so wide, for they looked first at each other and then at me, as if seeking an explanation. From the shore you can't see the road or the lower storeys. With the perspective of the view from below, my know-all's window on the third floor suddenly struck me as even more know-all and unattractive.

With the withdrawal of the water, cleaner pebbles had now appeared. On the edge, ants swarming over a tyre. Bits of crockery that had slid down from the dump on the slope. A stovepipe full of holes. Two young children wandering, looking for whelks among the broken glass that shines like spangles. A big stick floating in the sea. A bit further on, a lengthening line of fuel oil. Towards mid-morning, the salty virginal smell of the sea is replaced by a mossy smell. There is an odd peace in this place, which makes the electricity of mother earth and the radiation of the sea feel more dense. A natural cosmic peace. The wake of a passing ship has suddenly struck the beach. Three oyster-catchers have abandoned themselves to the waves like hollow toy ducks and are bobbing up and down, taking it easy.

My eye has lighted on a tortoise, upside-down on the beach and vainly struggling. No doubt the mischievous work of those two children. They are further along now, playing ducks and drakes. In the world of animals there is pitiless annihilation. There is savagery. But mankind alone has a gift for torture, the deliberate infliction of pain, and of the most excruciating kind. I turned the tortoise up into its natural position. If it weren't shrunk into its shell I would have kissed its hand and apologized on behalf of the children. At these hours the rocks don't get many patrons. A pelican, finding them vacant, has come and settled on one. It is smearing its beak with the secretion of its tail and rubbing its back.

The tortoise has started to walk on in its bandy-legged way, as if nothing had happened, not giving a damn for anything. Every so often it stops, for no apparent reason, then walks on again. The sun has thoroughly warmed the beach. The tortoise has passed by the massed ants, taking no notice of them. Now it has encountered a snail by the tyre; it hasn't acknowledged that either. Clearly it thinks of nothing but enjoying the sunshine. It keeps on walking, as if listening out for something. Do tortoises need to think? I don't suppose so. If they had any thoughts they wouldn't be so attractive. No, tortoises don't think, they have no prejudices or hindsights. The tortoise is unacquainted with the chain of cause and effect. Why does it exist? Why, though it live for a hundred or a hundred and fifty years, will it one day cease to be? Why has it been created stuck in its shell? It doesn't know that either. It exists because it exists. It's been created with its shell because that's how it's been created. It walks because it walks, it stops because it stops. It has no self-doubt. The inferiority complex and what is thought to be its converse but is in fact the same, the superiority complex, have never come its way. Nor is it concerned with 'Do they see me? What do they think of me?'

Ah, I tell you there is a whole world on the beach. On this beach there is no room for people with their noses in the air, people who think they know everything. It is the land of the

96

humble in heart, the land where nothing is valid but natural habit. Simply living. No drawing of conclusions, no forming of interpretations. No attaching of labels such as yesterday, the day before, today, tomorrow, the day after. Simply living. With no abstract speculation, never presuming to show off. Recognizing the right to life of every creature of nature, blending with them all, able to be content with being one of their number. Not talking, not writing, not making oneself conspicuous, not worrying or caring about the judgments of others.

Would you say that the best course is to put into practice this lesson in ecology which the beach teaches? Or to go up, now to the terrace, now to the street and the ground floor, now to the know-all third floor, but mostly to come down to this beach and, through the amalgam of these descents and ascents, these comings and goings which put one in mind of the electric current alternating between the clouds and the tortoise, to look forward to reaching somewhere else, somewhere more interesting?

The Statue

[Another timeless story, this one written in 1945.]

I want a statue put up to me. That's not a crime, is it? Everybody's got some weakness, some fancy, and this is mine. And I suppose more or less every great man has a desire to see himself reproduced in bronze. Otherwise would they ever be willing to sacrifice their valuable time to pose for hours in front of sculptors? Of course they wouldn't. That means I'm not the only one with a taste for this sort of thing. Still, I'm a modest chap, so I'm not going to put up my statue in one of the public squares of the city. Mine's going to be rather more of a private monument. It's going to be put up in a garden.

My business colleagues to whom I've spoken of my intention give me funny looks and don't say anything. All the same, there are quite a few smart alecs who can be very tactless. According to them, I'm not sufficiently important to have a statue put up to me. I'd do better to abandon this lunatic notion. And so on, and so on. Naturally, I pay no attention to them; I just smile and carry on my way. What can you call it but jealousy and envy?

For thirty years I've been in the Angora wool trade. Never, in the world of commerce or in my private life, have I committed a single act that might impair my honour and good name. I can produce hundreds of witnesses to the fact that I am an honest businessman. My reputation in the commercial world is as it should be. I'm a wholesaler. Before the War I used to export to Germany. Now it's mostly England we do business with. Anyway, what I'm trying to say is I'm not just anybody. Collected in my person I have all the virtues necessary for having a statue erected to me. If it's fame that's wanted, go to Bahchekapi and mention Uryanizade Sidki; you'll find no one there who doesn't know me. Wealth? Thank God I've that too. I haven't worked it

98

out myself but the Inland Revenue reckon I've a million and a half. Being of use to the country? Likewise. I have served my country in the economic field to the utmost of my ability, by perceiving the value of one of our national assets, making it known abroad and thus earning foreign currency for the State. What more can you ask?

I considered the matter and everything seemed in order. First of all I looked for a suitable place for the statue. The front garden of my apartment-house in Shishli struck me as appropriate. It's a bit on the small side but it looks onto the main street, where there's a lot of coming and going. I thought that was a good idea, so that the people passing by could see it. Besides, from the window of my first-floor flat I could view it all the time. Having fixed the place for it, I consulted a friend who understands these matters, and asked him about a good sculptor. He gave me three names. I got my secretary to invite them all to the office and explained the problem.

All three of them were sensible, well-bred young men. They agreed to do the statue. I was meaning to put the work out to tender, but the sculptors saw no need for that; they came to an arrangement among themselves and undertook the commission jointly. I wasn't stingy about the price. Well, you know, I've a fair bit of experience in this sort of thing. If you stint, in the end you come out the loser. The chaps will feel aggrieved and the statue will turn out shabby and inglorious. You get what you pay for. Anyway, we agreed on seven thousand liras. They would provide the bronze and all the bits and pieces; everything bar the pedestal.

I began calling at the studio to sit for them, for an hour or so of an evening on the way home from the office. First of all, the statue is made from clay. Then they take the mold and cast it in bronze. The sculptors thought I was an admirable type. 'We've been making statues all these years,' they said, 'and this is the first time we've come across anyone like you.' Yes, seriously, I suppose that's the way I am. So indeed Refik the rope-merchant, the man in the office next to mine, often says, 'You have an air of command. You were wrong to go into business. You were clearly cut out for the Army.'

This awe-inspiring look is a gift I was born with. Mind you, the science of sculpture has advanced so much now that these magical chaps can, if they like, make the most utter clod come out in the finished product looking like a hero. You look, and lo and behold some glassy-eyed imbecile has suddenly assumed the face of a genius; with beetling brow and broad vision he looks down on the world.

About six years ago I went on a business trip to Hungary. That was my first sight of Europe, so everything aroused my admiration. But what interested me most was the statues that adorned the streets. I studied every last one of them. Most were on horseback, hand on sword-hilt, men of majesty. Then a thought came to me. Their impressive bearing owed as much to those exaggerators we call sculptors as it did to the heroic postures they had struck and the high pedestals on which they were set. All of them, I am sure, were basically people like you and me. But take a look at their statues. They have a lofty bearing, as if they were not of our kind, as if they had not lived like us, had never mooched about the streets in search of amusement, had never eaten and drunk or, after eating, picked their teeth and belched, nor ever sworn when they were angry. It's false, you may be sure; quite false. If the sculptors had shown them open-mouthed and snoring or, I don't know, picking their noses, instead of the way they do, on horseback and all that, there wouldn't be anything left of that awe-inspiring majesty. When I told my sculptors this idea of mine, they laughed.

'You're right,' they said. 'But, for a statue to be a statue, it has to freeze one aesthetic moment; the pose has to bear an heroic impression.'

In fact I'd told them that just for something to say, to show them I'd got a bit of a clue about art. I take it that my statue will be a thing of fame and glory, like the rest of them. It's always been so and that's how it'll go on. We too shall conform to the fashion. In any case, if a person's innately awe-inspiring, like me, it doesn't make any difference what pose he assumes; he can sit in his underwear and he still won't lose any of his awesomeness.

A good job, says the old proverb, takes forty days. Mine

took a hundred and forty. One Thursday evening I was invited to the studio, *en famille*. When the sculptors drew the curtain covering the statue, the view that confronted me struck me all of a heap. To be absolutely honest with you, a shudder went down my spine. My wife's eyes were moist with emotion. The children were transfixed with astonishment.

The statue is one and a half times life-size. I am standing, one foot a little forward of the other. I am gazing into the distance, and my head is slightly turned to one side. One hand is on my hip, the other hangs down, loose. A majestic attitude. I don't begrudge a penny of what it's costing me. It has turned out exactly as I had wished.

I had paid half the fee in advance and I handed over the balance that very same day. But I had to leave the statue in the studio for a while longer, as the pedestal I was having built in the garden wasn't yet finished. In fact all the snags rose from that pedestal.

One morning I saw two council officials in our garden, talking to the workmen. Then the janitor came and said they wanted to see me. The moment they came in, they asked, 'This thing you're constructing in the garden; what is it?'

'It is the pedestal of my statue,' I replied.

Thereupon the shorter one of the two turned to the other and gave him a look indicating something like 'Aha! So it's true!' He then addressed himself to me again. 'Were you not aware that the requirements of the new city plan are that no construction be carried out on this street and that council permission must be obtained for the erection of statues?' I knew nothing of the kind.

'Since that is the procedure,' I said, 'I shall make an application and obtain permission.'

'Until that happens,' they replied, 'you will kindly halt the construction.'

'Very well,' I said.

Next morning I went to the Town Hall in person. I gave the requisite application to the Deputy Mayor. 'Your proposal will be examined,' said he, and dismissed me. A fortnight later I called again. They got rid of me; the

Governor, it seemed, was busy. I tried again in a month. They put me off: 'The matter is still under scrutiny and a decision is not yet possible.'

Finally I could stand it no longer. I insisted on seeing the Governor. As ill luck would have it, it seemed he was not in his office that day. I dug my toes in. 'I'll wait till he comes,' I said. While we were wrangling like that, a door opened and a man with white hair stuck his head out. He asked the reason for the noise and they told him. This aristocratic-looking person I subsequently discovered to be one of the most influential members of the City Council.

He obviously knew all about it, for he said, 'Ah! That statue business?' Then he took me into a lounge and smilingly indicated a chair. He offered me a cigarette too. He sat down facing me and began.

'I gather you want to erect a statue of yourself. It would never cross my mind to put obstacles in the way of anyone's wishes. And whether or not this is the time to undertake such an outlay is doubtless something you yourself will know best. But if, with the money you're laying out for this statue, you were to build a hospital ward or, say, a school or something like that, in my opinion you would have done something more worthwhile. Your name would be perpetuated and the country would benefit.'

'You are right, sir,' I replied. 'This matter apart, my greatest ambition is to perform some work of charity, as you suggest, in the area of social assistance. But the statue in question is now done and finished and paid for, so if there is no objection . . .'

At that point he cut me short. 'Done and finished?' he murmured. 'Extraordinary! All right, and what is it like? Big? Small? A bust? A statue?'

'It's big, quite big. One and a half times life-size.'

'My dear sir! Can I be hearing you correctly? If it were small, well, that wouldn't be so bad. But here you are saying it's big. If you put it up on the street, the people passing by would see it and it would attract attention.'

'But my dear sir! That is why I want it! Or does the law not allow it?'

'No, it's not that. Unfortunately (I am quoting his exact words) I have been unable to find any relevant provision in the Municipal Code. The matter of erecting statues in private buildings has not been considered; there are merely a number of special provisions about statues to be put up in public open spaces. It is quite true there is nothing about this in the law, but when the tastefulness of the urban environment comes into question the right to rule on the matter belongs to the City Council. And the ruling may go against you.'

'Most peculiar! I don't understand; this isn't something that would spoil the tastefulness of the urban environment. It's a work of art. A work of art created at a cost of seven thousand liras.'

'As I have indicated, if we treat this as a legal matter, both you and the Council will waste time with a mass of formalities, to no purpose. If we were to make this request of you privately, would you, I wonder, be so good as to agree? Please, my dear sir, don't put up that statue there. Just think for a moment. Suppose, as there's nothing about it in the law, everyone who takes a fancy to do so goes and puts up a statue of himself in front of his house, what will Istanbul come to look like? Tourists who visit the city will be taken aback at the sight of this bewildering variety of monuments, won't they? And will we not have thereby diminished the value of our real memorials?'

'I cannot share your view,' I said. 'For one thing, not everybody who would like to put up a statue of himself can do so. It's a question of financial resources. For another, even if someone were intending to have a statue of himself made . . .'

Once more the fellow interrupted me. 'That means you're going on with it. Very well, we shall just submit the problem to the City Council and notify you of the result.' So saying, he rose to his feet and I had no option but to leave.

I waited a month, two months, three months, then a fourth. No notification came or anything else. Meanwhile the sculptors kept telling me to get the statue out of the studio. I saw no way round it, so I rented a truck and had the statue brought home. As a temporary measure I put it in the paved courtyard. Without a pedestal, of course. For the moment I could show it only to visitors. Well, it's no use crying over spilt milk but the other day my son was playing ball and knocked the whole great thing over. When I got home in the evening and saw the head of the statue broken off at the neck and the lovely paved courtyard in fragments, I saw red. But we couldn't possibly have had the statue standing inside the house, and obviously something like this was bound to happen. Should I be grieving at the waste of so much money or at the fact that this business has made me into a laughing-stock? And while I was lamenting on these lines, my brother-in-law, who was visiting us that evening, jumped in with a suggestion.

'Don't upset yourself,' he said. 'Every cloud has a silver lining, and I've just had a thought. Why wouldn't the city let you put this statue up? It was because it was too big, wasn't it? But if you get some shoulders made and use it as a bust, they won't object. You know there's that bust of Tevfik Fikret in the garden of Galatasaray School. You can perfectly well put up something like that.'

An agreeable suggestion, it seemed to me. 'Right,' I said. 'And what about the torso? What shall we do with that?'

'You leave that to me. I'll flog it for a reasonable price, either to Istanbul City Council or to some town out in the sticks. All they'll have to do is fix a head on top and it'll make a lovely monument to someone or other.'

The Auction

I seem to spend my life at exhibitions. Exhibitions of pictures, sculpture, ceramics, handicrafts: you name it, I go to it. Do I go and buy? Certainly not. All I do is look my fill and lament. Yes, that is precisely the word for it, I lament. I look and look and I grieve over the items that have been bought. I grieve; yes, that's the more appropriate term. When I see a picture, a rug, a vase, a – oh, I don't know, a trinket, which has found favour with someone, reserved, a deposit paid on it, the purchaser's name and address stuck on the bottom in case someone else should lust after it. I am overwhelmed with grief. I am filled with rancour for the one who has bought it. I am immediately infuriated. Whoever the buyer may be, that lawyer, engineer, contractor, doctor, businessman or whatever, I regard his putting his label there as a kind of superfluous showing-off.

What it conveys is this: 'You see that vase, the one over there, with my visiting-card next to it? I've bought it, friend. I am So-and-so, the building contractor. My address is in the lower left corner of the card. Flat number such-and-such in the Günnur Apartments at Ayazpasha. My telephone number, 49.99.96. That's where I'm taking this vase. I shall embellish it with the flowers of my choice. It is mine now, and although you may want it you cannot buy it. It is not for you. Curse your fate and reconcile yourself to the fact that you are a wimp, right?'

That vase has gone to him now, and yet another mad yearning has started up inside me. Why didn't I come sooner? I didn't see it. I got there first, before the customer who wanted it, but I didn't want it. At one point I decided on it; why did I then change my mind? Do you see what's happened? That thrice-accursed clod has bought it and carried it off. Now you can eat your heart out!

Yet the fact is that yesterday I passed it by. I suppose it was because it was ownerless that I attached no importance to it. I suppose I did not sufficiently take in its beauty, its specialness. Even if I did, I suppose the reason I did not fall upon it was that I thought, 'There it stands; I can buy it whenever I like.' Moreover, the owner of the gallery kept pressing me: 'Listen to me, my friend, I'm telling you to buy it. It would be a sin to let it go to somebody who doesn't appreciate it.' And the little vase itself, squeaking in distress, waited for me to buy it. But I was being got at, you see. I felt that I had all I wanted; disdain set in, a lack of interest, a desire to make any excuse not to buy it, a determination to ascribe to the vase all manner of faults. Oh no, the colour was a bit too light. Oh no, there was some surplus glaze on the edge. I the simpleton, I the mug, kept fobbing the man off with such remarks as 'Do you *really* think the colours won't blister and rub off when you put water in it?' and 'It hasn't been fired, friend. In two years' time, these varnishes are going to craze, aren't they?'

The more he praised the vase, and the more the little vase looked deep into my eyes, saying 'Buy me!', the more I feigned a lack of interest. And when they kept on at me, I just said, 'Even if I wanted it, I couldn't buy it. It's the end of the month, you know; I've got no money,' and ran off. Three cheers for freedom of choice!

'All right,' you may say, 'then forget about it.' Well, I can't; such is my damnable disposition. Will that man who bought it appreciate it? Will he manage to pick a good place for it? The vase will look incongruous even in his hand. The half-wit won't know how to hold it; he'll hold it like an illiterate holding a newspaper. Wherever he puts it, the poor little vase will feel out of place. Look at it! Fine as crystal! The fellow will tread on it. He'll misuse it. It had the beginnings of a crack anyway, and he'll crack it right through. Perhaps he'll smash it. Whereas if I had bought it, I would have handled it gently. I would have taken it home and put it on my desk, and on the bedside table at night. I would have cherished it and would never have left it without flowers at any season of the year.

Now, having turned my back on a vase which was mine for the taking, and having let someone else grab it, why should I feel as though it had been stolen from me? Because of my rotten disposition.

For a man of such a disposition, can any place be imagined more distressing, more mortifying, than an auction room? What does an auction mean but having to endure seeing some article, which you could not make up your mind quickly enough to buy, bid up and carried off before your very eyes by other people?

I could tell you that it must be this feeling that has hitherto kept me from attending auctions. But I shan't. Nor do I want to. I don't myself know what I want to say. Because I am not yet sure that this is the real reason that has kept me away from auctions. The funny thing is that I am not sure that I am not sure about this. Basically, I do not myself believe what I say. Nor can I decide what I ought to believe.

Exhibitions and auctions aside, I am not at all jealous. Goethe, the teacher of us all, said, 'There's nothing clever in sharing other people's sorrows. What is really difficult is being able to take pleasure in other people's success, being able to participate wholeheartedly in their happiness.' You may ask my friends and acquaintances: they will not find it easy to point to anybody else who is as foolishly pleased as I, yes, most sincerely as I, at other people's success and good luck. I am not boasting. In a world where everyone throws mud at everyone else's eyes, this may be called foolishness or idiocy. And although it ought to be wrong to call it by these names, the unpleasant truth is that it may be right.

But at exhibitions and auctions the case is different. It is as though I have reserved purely for these contexts my stock of jealousy, which I never use in my working life, in my profession or in the field of art.

Nor is it correct to call this emotion jealousy. I use the word here because we have no other word to express the shade of meaning. For jealousy is above all a selfish emotion, whereas this lamentation of mine is not on my behalf but on behalf of things which are unappreciated and likely to remain so. Am I succeeding in explaining myself, I wonder? I see I'm not. The best thing will be to get on with the story.

The flat was by no means small, but we could not find room to put our feet. The weather was not at all hot, but we were pouring with sweat.

The auctioneer's man, standing on a chair, was shouting, 'Lot 77. Card table and four padded chairs, plastic throughout. Worth a hundred and fifteen liras. I'm starting at one hundred.'

I was surrounded by well-off people. Newly-weds arm in arm, engaged couples about to set up house, gentlemen with cigars, ladies in fur coats. And what have I come in search of, in this galère?

In particular, there is a well-dressed man next to me, in his fifties, smoking a pipe, grey-haired, like an English lord. When our eyes met, I didn't know where to put myself. He gave me a disparaging look that got on my nerves, the sort first-class passengers give the passengers in steerage.

'Who do you think you are, coming here?' said the look. 'How much money have you in your pocket? None of us has ever seen you here. Who are you? Who are your family? Ah, of course, you're not a buyer, you're a spectator. You don't look much like a buyer. You read the advertisement in the newspaper on Sunday morning. You wondered what this thing they call an auction might be like, so you got up and came here. Well, given that you've come, should you not at least have had a shave before showing yourself in front of all these people? In Europe, even the commonest workman pays a bit of attention to his appearance on Sundays. I can't see your shoes very well in this crush, but I'll bet they're old and haven't been polished. Ah yes. You are embarrassed when people look too hard at you. Well, you're here now, so watch. What's that you said? Who am *I*? You can tell who I am from this pipe-tobacco of mine. It's specially made in England; they steep it in honey and wine. Do you get the fragrance of the smoke? You do. Look, I bought this pipe in Liverpool, for four pounds sterling. Everybody is good at something. I, my friend, am an expert in making money and living well. You look like the sort of know-all who passes for a philosopher. I get terribly angry with people like that. Because you can't make money, you have to console yourself by despising and jeering at those who can. If, instead of expending your intellect on juggling with words, you were to expend it on positive, lucrative activities, you'd never come here on a Sunday morning dressed like that and with a face like that. Can you tell the Waldstein Sonata played by Wilhelm Kempff from the same sonata played by Gieseking? I can. Do you know that roast beef tastes different when it's eaten with a silver knife and fork? What is the difference between calvados and brandy? Is the Cadillac or the Rolls-Royce the more comfortable car? There, I'm deliberately asking you the easy ones, and still you can't guess the answers. You see, my friend, life consists in these small *nuances*, in the *raffinement* which distinguishes them. I have an instinct, a kind of *Fingerspitzengefühl*, for such things. I fear you understand nothing of what I am saying.'

Well, I do understand, for what it's worth. Most people get angry with the sort of rich man – precisely your sort – who is knowledgeable, has taste, and is capable of savouring life. With the other sort, one can console oneself with the thought that the fellow may be a millionaire but he is also a clod. But don't worry, my Europeanized friend. I am not irritated by either sort.

The auctioneer, whose name, it appears, is Portakal, is shouting: 'Lot number 78. A miracle of American technology. One Montgomery automatic sofa, turns into a bed when required. Complete with mattress. Worth eight hundred liras, we're starting at seven hundred and fifty.' Then to his assistant who conducts the actual bidding, 'Right! Off you go!'

'Seven hundred.'

'And ten.'

'Fifteen.'

'Twenty.'

'Seven hundred and twenty I am bid.'

'Thirty.'

'Forty.'

'Let's go up in tens, gentlemen. Quickly now.'

'You've got fifty.'

'Sixty.'

'We're at seven hundred and sixty.'

'Ninety.'

'Jolly good!'
'Ninety-five.'
'A hundred and ten.'
'Thirty.'
'Thirty-five.'
'We're at eight hundred and thirty-five, one Montgomery automatic sofa, turns into a bed when required.'
'Eight hundred and forty.'
'Make it fifty.'
'Seventy. Oh, is it you? Nice to see you, Mr Albert.'
'Nice to be here.'
'Seventy-five.'
'Eighty.'
'Ninety.'
'Ninety-five.'
'That's eight hundred and ninety-five. How are you, Hafiz?'
'Fine, thanks, and you?'
'Nine hundred.'
'Nine hundred and ten!' This from a stout, crew-cut man across the room.
'Any advance on nine hundred and ten, gentlemen? Going, going . . . Hikmet Bey, do you want it? Bid.'
Hikmet Bey, it seemed, was the English lord in front of me, the one smoking honey-flavoured tobacco. Everybody was looking at Hikmet Bey.
'Do you want it, Hikmet Bey? Bid.'
Hikmet Bey simply lowered his left eyebrow, meaning, 'Up!'
'Nine hundred and twenty here.'
This time, all eyes were on the previous bidder, the man with the crew-cut. And his blood was up. Well, it would be, wouldn't it? 'Nine hundred and thirty!' he shouted.
The auctioneer's man looked at Hikmet Bey. Again his left brow descended. 'Forty,' said the assistant. He was as proud as if he himself were bidding.
The crew-cut man was quite carried away. 'Fifty,' he said.
Was there anything more to say? His face had gone as red as a cock's comb. Let's see what Hikmet Bey's going to do.

110

Yes, again he dropped his left eyebrow.

'I have sixty here,' said the auctioneer's man.

The crew-cut man was very cross indeed. But he stopped and thought, and put the brake on hard. 'Let him have it,' he said.

The Montgomery sofa was knocked down to Hikmet Bey. It was obvious anyway that Hikmet Bey was a redoubtable man. I looked closely. He was quite unruffled; not a hair had stirred. The crew-cut citizen, on the other hand, had gone bright purple with excitement. Hikmet Bey is an old hand at this game. He doesn't tire himself. He never joins in the first stages of the bidding. When the bidders are eliminated one by one, he is left in single combat with the most eager of them. After that, the auctioneers keep their eyes on him. While other bidders are agonizing, suddenly he brings down his left eyebrow. 'Up! Up! Up! That's enough.'

When he secured the lot, he did not rejoice and preen himself as others would have done. Quietly he slipped Mr Portakal the three hundred liras deposit. So he had come there simply to buy that Montgomery sofa. Yes, he gave some sort of instructions to Mr Portakal and went.

This Mr Hikmet must come here often. Consider, they know him by name and are aware of what he wants and what he doesn't want.

I took careful note. When you get down to it, the biggest spenders tend to be people like that, quiet, not making a fuss, sure of themselves, knowing what they are going to buy and how much they are going to pay for it.

At that point my eye fell on a short, fat lady who was standing against the far wall, beside the auctioneers. Would you believe it, she smiled. It had to be at me. If Hikmet Bey were still there, I would have said it was at him. But Hikmet Bey had gone. I turned and looked behind me. The people behind hadn't even noticed. The woman was smiling broadly at my puzzlement. She waved. I waved back. Ah! Now I recognize her. It'll be her; yes, it is her. When I was living at Salajak, my landlady had a daughter. They say one forgets the name of one's first love. Was it Fahrünnisa? Nurunnisa? Something of that kind. Oh the dear old days! I had run into

111

her again once, ten years ago. Since then she had turned into
a barrel. But how slim she had been in the old days! We used
to go to the far end of the iron jetty that ran out to sea, and
recite sad poems to each other. She was very romantic. 'I
want my husband to be an invalid,' she would say. 'I want to
sit by him and look after him.' If her husband were ill now,
would this woman give him so much as a spoonful of soup?
But her husband is scarcely likely to be ill. He'll be rubicund
and smiling, like her. Her hands don't look as though she did
a lot of work. They must have a cook. Or they eat out.

My plump beloved keeps on smiling. Maybe if the room
were not so crowded she would come over to me. She points
me out to the girl next to her. Her daughter? Yes, that's it.
When I saw her ten years ago, she had a primary-school girl
with her. A man can tell he's getting old when he sees the
marriageable daughters of his old flames. My one-time beloved pointed me out to her daughter, who scrutinized me
and smiled politely. Fahrünnisa was giving me a significant
look. Although she was approaching forty, there still re-
mained a certain something in her eyes.

The ocular conversation went like this:

'You remember the old days, don't you?'

'Can I ever forget?'

'Oh you, you!'

'You were quite something too, my darling Fahrünnisa.'

At the same time, though, her eye was on the vacuum
cleaner, and the message was clear: 'When that lot comes up,
let me not miss it.'

A sudden regret flooded my being. Why had I come here
today so scruffily dressed and, moreover, so badly in need of
a shave? You see? Just my luck that I should run into an old
heart-throb. A man may relax by going round scruffily
dressed, like a vagrant. I do not dispute it. And let us grant
that he is, to a certain extent, at liberty to shave or not to
shave. But he ought to make every effort to tidy himself up
before going to places where old sweethearts might be,
simply so as not to spoil the poetry of their memories, not to
make them ashamed of what has been. We should be at least
as respectably dressed as their present husbands, and we

should take care not to appear elderly, grey-haired, seedy, or penurious.

Fahrünnisa is bound to be pitying me now. She is thinking, 'Oh these men!' My beloved from Üsküdar is bound to be thinking this, I know. 'Look at him going around like a tramp. Look at that face, he hasn't shaved for days. But if we had married, I would have kept him in order. If he were ill, I would have looked after him (you remember that she had a fancy for tending the sick). In short, I would have made a man of him. I am in part responsible for his rake's progress. Maybe it was because I married someone else and left him that he has lost interest in life and has let himself go.'

She is pointing me out to her daughter and saying something. The daughter has looked at me. She is smiling. Her mother makes a gesture which means, 'My daughter, you see. She's as tall as I am.'

More ocular conversation:

'God bless her. She is like a young gazelle. Whose daughter is she, my love?'

'Oh you brute! How can you be so detached?'

Again her eyes turned to the vacuum cleaner. If she doesn't get it, I shall be sorry too.

My beloved from Üsküdar is saying, 'One.'

When the assistant says, 'A hundred and twenty,' she says 'One.'

'A hundred and twenty-five.'

'One.'

So this is her auction technique. Clearly very tight-fisted. What a difference from Hikmet Bey, going up ten liras at a time! And no signalling with the eyebrow, either. Fahrünnisa calls out like a corncrake.

At one point she said, 'I shan't buy it. Let it go.'

The others go on bidding.

'A hundred and eighty.'

'Eighty-five.'

'Ninety.'

Would you believe it, she jumps back in. 'One!'

I thought she'd given up. But it seems she only pretends to give up, so as to wear out the opposition. This is another subtlety of her tactics. To cut a long story short, the vacuum cleaner was knocked down to her. Well done, Fahrünnisa! She is another resolute buyer, like Hikmet Bey. Never mind that their techniques are somewhat different; look at the results. She takes out her bag and pays a deposit, and then comes a surreptitious glance round, to see if they are looking at her. She's the archetypal Provincial Governor's wife. Governor of somewhere at the back of beyond, he may be, but she's a Governor's wife. Governor of one of the eastern provinces, he may be, but she's a Governor's wife. Neither her paste ring nor the huge earrings can diminish her imposing presence.

The assistant had got down from the chair. There was a move towards the other room; the furnishings of the small drawing-room were about to be auctioned. At this point I found my plump sweetheart at my side. 'A strange coincidence,' she said, 'isn't it?'

'Very.'

'How long is it since last we talked?'

'It must be ten years since I saw you, fifteen since we talked.'

'What! Oh the good old days,' said Fahrünnisa. 'They really were great days.'

'Yes, they were.'

'Are you still writing poetry?'

'Dear me, no! That's all over and done with.'

She laughed. 'Don't tell me your source of inspiration dried up?'

Her lipstick had left a pink stain on her front teeth. My source of inspiration! How nice! 'Could be,' I said. I was about to say, 'Now I've seen you, I may start writing again,' but I thought that a married woman might not like that, in the presence of her daughter.

The daughter was a pretty little thing, just like all the other girls. She had met a friend, and was talking to her.

'Do you ever go to the old place?' asked Fahrünnisa.

'Never,' I said. 'Since that time I haven't been able to go back.'

Without being aware of it, and certainly without meaning

to, I must have said that in a sad tone. 'Why?' she asked, fluttering her false eyelashes. I knew what was going through her mind; she was thinking that she was not making my heart beat faster. It was incumbent on me to heave a sigh and to say, 'I don't know.' I did so. 'Maybe,' I said, 'I am afraid of going back to the old memories.'

Just give Fahrünnisa a chance to get sentimental! 'I confess that I have sometimes felt the same thing.'

I was suddenly frightened, in case she might make other confessions. I felt the need to introduce something prosaic into the conversation, which was becoming too romantic for my liking. 'You really did get that vacuum cleaner cheap.'

She suddenly awoke from her reverie. 'Last week I missed getting one even cheaper. This one's a bit of a swindle. The Americans have learned all about the market. They've become tradesmen. If you knew what bargains there used to be in the early days!'

She knew this business inside out. It may be that she bought things cheaply at the sales and resold them privately. I have heard that some wide-awake ladies are doing this. I don't know if it was because she divined my thoughts that she said, 'Füsun is getting married. We're putting together a few oddments for her. For weeks we've been after a refrigerator. And now I hear that the Gibson they have here doesn't work properly. Nizamettin says we should buy a new one. Prices have gone up, you know; the new tinny ones cost the earth. I say it ought to be an old one, they're better. What have you come to buy?'

'Me?' I said. 'There's a bamboo suite I thought I'd have a look at.' What would I be doing with a bamboo suite? But at that moment my self-respect needed a lie of that sort. More accurately, not my self-respect but Fahrünnisa's. Yes, that's it, Fahrünnisa's self-respect. 'But I don't like it,' I went on. After that sentence there was no alternative but to shut up.

'You're right,' said my plump love. 'It's very common; I didn't fancy it either. The week before last, Ilhami the engineer and his wife snapped up a lovely bamboo suite. You should have seen it. Aren't your buying anything else?'

'I don't know, I'm thinking.'

115

There are ten days till the end of the month. In my pocket I have eighty-one liras. What can I buy? But then it struck me that it was impossible for me to have come to this flat today to buy nothing, and equally impossible for me, in the presence of Fahrünnisa and her daughter, to leave it without buying something, especially as I had come looking so scruffy and unprepossessing. This was a woman who, fifteen years before, had loved me or had pretended to love me or may just have seemed to love me. I could not appear in her eyes as a layabout who had come to the American auction merely to kill time on a Sunday.

But what on earth am I to buy? I cannot buy the Rever radio with tape recorder, which has a reserve of two thousand seven hundred liras. I cannot buy the seven-foot Gibson refrigerator at two thousand five hundred. Or the metal desk at two thousand, or the three armchairs at fifteen hundred, or the automatic sofa-bed at a thousand. Nor can I buy the silver cutlery, the cut-glass cups and bowl, or the Sèvres dinner-service. I can't even buy the Zenith radio, the ash-wood dresser, or the forty-five record-player. If I can buy anything at all from here it will be a couple of classical long-play records for twenty liras each. Maybe a few books. As the man is an American and a businessman, he is bound to have Dale Carnegie's books on his shelves. I shall play the records and learn to distinguish Wilhelm Kempff from Gieseking. I shall open the books, to save myself from being a mere pretender to culture, and I shall exercise my brains in pursuit of the positive, like Hikmet Bey, and learn to grow rich. One more year, and I'll come here not to daydream but to lower my left eyebrow and buy Montgomery sofas, bamboo patio furniture, and imitation Matisses.

Yes, I had to do something, I had to join in a contest, I had to buy something, good or bad, as far as my money would reach. But at that moment I learned, from the conversation of the two people next to me, that the records were to be sold as one lot. So that door of hope was closed.

Over there, the books have come up. Portakal was shouting, 'Latest model Littré dictionary. Five volumes. Complete with supplement. It's worth sixty liras, we're starting at fifty.'

I've been looking for a Littré for ages. This will be killing two birds with one stone. I call out, 'Fifty-five.'

My voice had come out louder than normal. Suddenly all eyes were turned on me. Was this a frivolous bid? This was the first they had heard from the cunning customer who all this time had been lying low and waiting. He was a scruffy-looking fellow, but you never can tell. Sometimes the most unlikely chaps, like this one, bide their time and then strike like lightning. Who might he be? He doesn't look very wealthy. If he had any money he would have snapped up that mahogany dining-room suite that went for three thousand nine hundred a little while back. He's intent on a book. A thing with tattered binding. An antique, do you think? The fellow must be a dealer in second-hand books.

'Fifty-five I am bid. It's worth sixty. Dictionary in five volumes.'

'Sixty,' said someone in the corner.

'Sixty-five,' I riposted.

You know how sometimes in the films all eyes are turned on a man who is winning heavily, has got chips piled up in front of him and says 'Bank for five million!' The men look at him enviously, the women admiringly and longingly. At that instant I had the illusion that that was happening to me. I could not look, but I felt I was being looked at. There was a moment when I encountered the caressing gaze – yes, caressing to my pride – of my plump sweetheart. Another conversation in the language of the eyes:

'You no longer care about poetry, but just look; you still care for books as you used to.'

'What would you, Fahrünnisa my darling? You left me, and so I devoted myself to books.'

'Seventy,' from another bidder.

I gather I have suddenly become a small-scale Hikmet Bey. The auctioneer's man doesn't know my name, but when I look at him after each bid, he looks at me. He is transforming me into a Hikmet Bey. So that this regard should not go for naught, I say, 'Seventy-one.'

'Two.'

'Three.'
'Five.'
'Eighty,' I shouted.
'Eighty,' the auctioneer's man repeated, looking at me, looking at me with respect and appreciation. 'Eighty,' he said again. Just as he was pleased and proud when Hikmet Bey bid up, so was he pleased and proud when I did. 'Eighty! Going, going, go . . .'

He was just saying '. . . ne' when, would you believe it, an uncouth voice from the rear said, 'Ninety.'

Everyone looked at the back of the room. It was one of those *nouveau riche* peasants, who couldn't even decipher the newspaper he was holding. He'd seen we were bidding and he no doubt thought, 'It must be some sort of antique; I'll buy it and put it aside.'

That's how it has always happened anyway, throughout my life. Every time the man is saying, 'Going, going, go . . . ,' and my hand is stretched out towards the article which is at last mine, some clod pops up and says, 'Ninety!' and my hand is left clutching thin air. All eyes turned towards the new bidder. A book which I have longed for for years and which no one would appreciate better than I, has been grabbed from under my very nose by an illiterate. So that he can read it? Not on your life. So that he can use the volumes as doorstops, or put them one on top of the other to climb up and reach the top shelf.

My plump beloved and her daughter, who for the last few minutes had been rooting for me, were now looking round sadly. Forgive me, Fahrünnisa. If I'd had another fifty liras on me, believe me, I'd have gone on bidding. I would even have paid two hundred and sixty for the dictionary that's worth sixty. Only so that you might be pleased. What rotten luck that it was the wrong end of the month. I've been bidding all my life and nothing has ever been knocked down to me. Was it likely that the Littré dictionary would be?

Then suddenly I cheered up. Maybe it's better this way. Keep bidding, but see that you're not left with it. Why, this fat woman whose favour I have once again lost, through failing to buy that book, wasn't she an article that at one time

I kept bidding for, but let someone else secure?

Do I regret it now? Far from it. On the contrary. Now I even feel sorry for the one who got her, the man I was angry at then. The luck of never yet having a lot knocked down to me is not to be despised. Sour grapes? No. Not at all. Absolutely not. When you get down to it, this may well be the most sensible course of conduct. Bid away, but don't end up with it. See what becomes of the lots you do end up with!

They can pity me behind my back as much as they like, with their 'He kept on bidding but he couldn't get it.' I, for my part, pity them. I can be considered the most fortunate man at this auction. Never mind about the Littré; suppose I were rich and had bought that mahogany dining-room suite, what would have happened? I would have paid the deposit on it and waited for the auction to end.

Let's pretend that that table, those chairs, that sideboard, which look so unbearably attractive to me because they are going to someone else, have been knocked down to me. I've paid the deposit, I've signed the invoice. They will settle down among my other possessions, they will sit there with the rest of my property, as burdensome and insipid as all acquisitions, with that meaningless, irritating confidence and stupid pride in having found an owner and seen their future secured.

Yes, if I had bought it, I would have waited for the auction to end, paid for it and seen my smug piece of property made over to me. All right, if you've nothing else to do you will have to look for porters, carts, trucks. When they realize the position, they will make heavy weather of it. They'll demand an arm and a leg. Let's say we've arranged terms. The stuff will be loaded onto the car-ferry and go over to the other side. It won't be possible to find room for it all, among the other furniture in the house. I shall have to get rid of some of the old things for a derisory price. I am bound not to feel at home with the newly-arrived furniture for a long time. Time will pass before I am used to it. One by one I shall see and learn those aspects of it which I failed to see in the turmoil of the first day, or which may even have struck me as beautiful.

And perhaps one day I shall regretfully say, 'What was I doing buying this suite?'

Whereas now I am as free as a bird. I can walk out of here any time I want. My hands in my pockets, my money in my wallet, I can whistle a tune and spend my afternoon wherever I like. No battling with porters, no wrangling with drivers. And my old table is perfectly sufficient for me. Anyway, the top of that sideboard was all scratched. Anyway, those plates were cracked. And, let's face it, wasn't that bed a monstrosity? My dear fellow, the bindings of the Littré were coming off; Larousse is perfectly adequate. My friend, that writing-desk was a vulgar thing.

The day we learn not to sigh after something that has gone, the day we find such consolations as these, or, if we cannot find them, invent them, on that day we may be considered as having mounted the first rung of the ladder of happiness.

Seeing that I have bought nothing, seeing that no lot has been knocked down to me, I can buy everything; every lot can be knocked down to me. I am free to choose. So long as I don't choose, I can be counted as luckier than all who have chosen. The one who makes his choice is in bondage. I wish him joy of his property.

It was at this point in my thinking, dear reader, yes, precisely at this point, that I realized I had never in all my life attended an auction with any inordinate desire inside me. I had never joined in the fray determined at all costs to buy something. What has kept me away from auctions has been no reason you might imagine other than this lack of decision. On that day, in that place, I understood for the first time – and I don't mean I seemed to understand, but that I understood as I understand that twice two is four – that if I wanted, if I decided, sooner or later I would get something. I would bid and all that, and if I was not successful in the bidding I would snatch the thing and run off, but I'd get something.

I am not one of those who bids and buys; I am just a loafer who plays at bidding. Then I sit down and have recourse to story-tellers' tricks, regurgitating tales of penury, and rubbish about being unlucky.

I now see this very clearly, as though I have directed a

searchlight into the basement of my consciousness.

I, who appear – indeed, who strive to appear – to be complaining that I keep bidding but always see the goods elude me, what have I ever taken seriously? What have I ever really been attached to?

If all the auctioneers and all the customers at an auction should ever unite and leave me in possession of some article which I have pretended to like and to bid for, I don't know what the hell I would do. Would I buy it? Would I be pleased? Or would I sulkily refuse to abide by the rules, and say, 'No, I shan't play with you any more. You've all ganged up to cheat me'? If telling a story is a form of confession, if I am an honest man, I can only answer, 'Yes, the latter is what I would do.'

In the same way that I brushed aside the vase and the gallery-proprietor I spoke of in the first lines of this story, throughout my life I have brushed aside all the vases and all the gallery-proprietors, all the lots and all the auctioneers.

Here is the sole truth I have managed to arrive at today, in the middle of my life. (Middle? It may be very close to the end of it.) I am a man who plays at auctions. Whatever I have so far taken hold of, I have never taken hold of as if it were for keeps, but with my fingertips, so as to be able to let go of it easily.

In order to preserve my freedom, fearing to be tied, I have taken care always to break away, to be able to break away.

'Twenty-five.'

Something's being auctioned over there.

My beloved from Üsküdar is after it. 'One.'

'Thirty.'

'One.'

'Forty. Forty over here.'

'One.'

'Forty-five. Do you want it, Hafiz Bey?'

'Eight,' said Hafiz Bey.

'Forty-eight I am bid.'

'I shan't buy it,' said Fahrünnisa. 'It's not worth it, let it go'.

'Going to Hafiz Bey for forty-eight, going, going, go . . .'

121

'Fifty,' I said, without knowing what was happening.

Again the eyes have turned on me. Fahrünnisa is staring in astonishment. Hafiz Bey too is taken aback. He stammers, 'Fifty-five.'

The auctioneer's man is looking at me.

'Sixty.'

'Sixty-five.'

'Seventy.'

'Eighty.'

Again the auctioneer's man is proud of me. Hafiz Bey hesitates. As well he might; I'm going up, Hafiz Bey, I'm going up.

He gulped, twice. 'Let it go.'

When Max Schmeling knocked out Joe Louis in the world heavyweight fight in 1936, he was not as pleased as I am now.

'At eighty, going to this gentleman, going, going, gone.

Gone indeed, Mr Auctioneer's Man. Just for the sake of the fitness of things, once in this life let me bid for something and buy it.

I handed over the money. They gave me my property. It turned out to be an iron-legged pedestal ashtray. I took it, and said quietly to Fahrünnisa, 'Will you accept this as a wedding present for your pretty daughter?'

Fahrünnisa's eyes shone. 'Oh I couldn't!' she said.

'Please!' I said. 'Don't reject it.'

'You're very kind,' she said. 'You can consider yourself her uncle.'

'On her mother's side,' I said, and made my farewell.

On my back the coat which I had lately had turned; inside me an enthusiasm for attending more auctions at which I would, as usual, buy nothing; on my lips a crooked smile which might have been due to sadness or to pleasure, swelling with pride I swaggered away from the auction.

Thickhead

[The term *besleme*, here rendered as 'fosterling', is applied to girls who are adopted into well-off households and perform domestic duties in exchange for their keep. In the fullness of time, the adopting families find husbands for them. This form of charity is still practised in Turkey. The only other note necessary is that the older cinemas in Istanbul do have boxes, like those in theatres.]

Who gave him this name, and when, nobody knows. But it fitted him so well that most people forgot his real name. At one time he worked as an apprentice in Feyzullah's café; the name may have been a relic of that period. You know there are silly people who enjoy giving nicknames to everyone they meet. One of them may have called him Thickhead just for something to say, just to annoy him and amuse himself at his expense, and it stuck. Or it may have been an addict of Sixty-six or some other card game, short-tempered because of a losing streak, who flew into a rage because he had ordered coffee and the boy didn't bring it soon enough, so he roared, 'What a thickhead that Kiazim is! The damned boy is good for nothing except gawping like an idiot!' After that it was 'Thickhead' all the time.

As I have indicated, a genuine thickheadedness was manifest in him. He was such a thickhead that he could not even get a place in our neighbourhood team, but always stood around as a reserve. Now that I mention the neighbourhood team, it occurs to me that the most likely explanation of the origin of his name is that it was given to him by a member of the team, precisely because he always stayed a reserve and never could get into the team.

If we had an away match, Thickhead would insist on tagging along. He would come with us and watch the game from behind the goal, longing for someone to be injured so that he could take his place. When someone was injured, that meant that the sun had risen for Thickhead. He would rush onto the field and, apparently thinking that any effort he put into playing was bound to achieve something, would even run after the ball if it went into touch and out of play. When what he was dreading finally happened, and the injured player came hobbling back onto the pitch after treatment, he would have to trot behind the goal once more. All he got out of it was ten minutes' play. In those ten minutes he would strain every nerve, take any risk, in the hope of attracting favourable attention and winning a place in the team. Often in an excess of enthusiasm he would charge the opposing forwards needlessly and cost us a penalty or two, and so lose us the game. For all that, he was not too bad a player. Although he committed purposeless fouls in his thirst for approbation, had he been able to play sensibly and intelligently like the rest, sure of his standing and his worth, he might very well have become a useful member of the team. For one thing, he had more puff than any of us. For another, once things started to get rough no one had more staying-power than Thickhead. By an odd chance, there were three left-handed brothers who played inside-left, outside-left, and left-back for Thunderbolt Sport – yes, Thunderbolt Sport; that was the name of our club. When they moved to another neighbourhood, among those taken into the team to fill the three vacancies was Thickhead.

Until then I had been playing in the team as right-half. Because Thickhead could not kick left-footed, they made him right-half and brought me to left-half, giving me no choice in the matter. You know of course that right-half and left-half are the most thankless positions in the team. They are the ones who work hardest, rush about the most, and are most fatigued. True, the centre-half gets just as tired as they do, but after all he is the centre-half, the backbone of the team. Nobody gives a damn for the right-half and left-half. The poor devils, pouring with sweat, are trying simultaneously to block the other team's inside-forwards and help their own forwards to attack, so they are worn to a frazzle. They get no recognition if the team wins. If it loses, everyone pitches into them. 'You stupid idiot,' they say, 'you didn't stop their inside-left.' 'If you'd marked their inside-right when he was moving across,' they say, 'we needn't have lost that second goal.' They say an awful lot of things. In short, being a right-half or left-half is a thankless task.

All the places in our team were bagged. Our goalie was a boy called Andon. He was a goalie who didn't care a damn for anyone or anything, and seemed to be made of india rubber. He used to do the most spectacular dives. He would stop the most unstoppable penalties, but sometimes you would see him beaten by the most unlikely shots at goal, which passed between his legs. Backs: Nejati, Little Nuri. Half-backs: Thickhead, Big Nuri, me. Forwards: Hikmet, Iska Fethi, Erjüment, Asim, Niko.

I had my eye on the position of outside-forward. Right or left, I didn't mind. But what chance did I have, when our outside-right, Hikmet, was the best player in the team? As for Niko, the outside-left, he wasn't in Hikmet's class, but he was an obstinate boy who kept insisting that he was going to stay at outside-left, and refused point-blank to play anywhere else. As he had the support of Erjüment, the team captain, there was nothing left for me but to go on being a lousy half-back.

Our team captain Erjüment was the son of a Member of Parliament, who paid for the balls and the strip. Erjüment had to stay at centre-forward, and if they wouldn't let him do so he would pick up his ball and his strip and go. Nor would he relinquish the captaincy to anyone else. The one who was indubitably entitled to it was Big Nuri, the centre-half, both because of his masterly playing and his seniority. But as I have said, it was a question of ball and strip.

Erjüment was attending the American College. He was a great show-off. He had a way of shaking hands with the opposing captain when they tossed, which was a sight to see. You would think he was Zeki Riza or Aslan Nihai. In fact he paid close attention to those men at league matches and memorized their mannerism one by one, from the way they came onto the field to the way they laced their boots; from the way they passed to the way they shot at goal. Then he would come to our neighbourhood pitch and inflict them on us.

All of Erjüment's football equipment was perfect. In this respect one could divide the members of the team into three categories. Some had nothing whatever, for example Andon, Little Nuri, and Thickhead. They used to play in their everyday boots and the strip they put on over their underwear or swimming-trunks. When the game warmed up, Thickhead went so far as to discard his shoes and play barefoot. He played better like that. Then came the half-equipped, those who, for the good of the team, shared a pair of boots with their friends. Thus all the players on the right wing had football boots on their right feet, ordinary shoes on their left feet, while all the left-wingers had football boots on their left feet and ordinary shoes on their right feet. Erjüment was our only player to wear football boots on both feet. In addition, inside his socks he used to put European shin-guards, bought from the National Sports shop, on his wrists snow-white wrist-straps, on his knees totally unnecessary rubber knee-protectors, and in that garb, hair meticulously combed, he would come out onto the pitch. In matches it was not his practice to tire himself overmuch, or to run energetically for passes, or to head the ball as it came off a corner-kick, for fear of disarranging his hair. But he would position himself neatly to receive convenient passes and, standing nearly but not quite offside, would produce goals we had no right to expect. In brief, we threw ourselves all over the pitch, stopped the other side's attacks, saved goals, got kicked in the groin, made all the preparations for our own attack and presented him with trouble-free passes. At the end of it, it was he who scored the goal and got the glory. If you are going to play at all, that's the way to play.

But I was going to tell you about Thickhead; I seem to have wandered off the point.

At the time when Thickhead Kiazim was playing half-back bare-foot for Thunderbolt Sport, he had long since resigned from his apprenticeship at the café and had gone in with Istepan the milkman. He worked on his dairy farm in winter, and in summer he made a living by selling newspapers and as a bootblack. Later he worked (in this order) as a fisherman at the Stockade, as a boatman at Kalamish, as a bus-conductor at Suadiye, and as a gardener in the Valdebagh Sanatorium. But being easily bored, he could never stick for more than three or four months, or six at the very outside, to any of the careers he kept taking up and dropping.

If one were to write a novel about Thickhead, each of the careers he tried could form a separate chapter of the work. Or it would be possible to write, not a novel, but a series of episodes, like the Karagöz shadow plays, with titles like 'Thickhead's Trip to Yalova', 'Thickhead on the Assault-craft', 'Thickhead the Night-Watchman', 'Thickhead in Tunis,' 'Thickhead Falls out with Lame Aziz', 'Thickhead the Fireman', 'The Marriage of Thickhead', and so on.

I am not intending to write either a novel or a story. What I want to do here is to project, as you might say, onto the white screen of the page, two or three takes extracted from different periods of his life and joined together, as though they were excerpts from a film.

I have said that Thickhead tried job after job. At one time he even worked as a waiter at the big restaurant at Jadde-bostan. But as he had always been accustomed to setting a high value on his personal dignity, he could not reconcile himself to the job one little bit. There was a conceited fool who wanted to show off to the girl he was with, so he tossed a tip in front of him as though giving alms to a beggar. If they hadn't held Thickhead back, he would have killed him. Of course he was sacked the next day. Whereupon he went off and signed on for national service. Ever since childhood, he had been very keen on the Navy. A Laz boy whom he knew from his days as a boatman had advised him, 'When they ask you your trade, say, "We've been boatmen for generations."' And indeed, when he told them he was a boatman they at once assigned him to the Navy.

After the first week, he put on his uniform and came visiting, like a child at festival time. He kept looking at himself surreptitiously in mirrors and shop windows. Every few minutes he would straighten his black kerchief, bend down and wipe the dust from his full trouser-legs, spit on any part of his clothing which was stained and clean it with his cuff. They put him in a torpedo-boat, and he was over the moon. He evidently had an enormous appetite for the service. Two months later, when the Aegean manoeuvres began, he kissed the hands of the elders of the neighbourhood as if he were going to a real war, and received their blessings. He embraced his coevals and they all declared that any scores they had against him were cancelled.

One Sunday after the manoeuvres were over, lo and behold, who should turn up but Thickhead? He had taken off the naval uniform he loved so well and was wearing a light-coloured suit; it was a little too big for him and consequently made him look very sloppy. He had on a brand-new raw silk shirt, a flashy tie with a pattern of twigs and flowers, on his right lapel a violet, on his left lapel the rosette of the Fener supporters' club. It was hard not to laugh.

Vakkas Bey the vet, more impatient than any of us, asked the question we were all dying to ask: 'What the hell are you ponced up like that for?'

Thickhead explained. It seems there was a lieutenant on the boat, who called him and said, 'Kiazim Efendi, there are quite a few ratings on this boat, but I reckon you are the pick of the bunch. I am going to send you to my aunt's house as an orderly. She lives in Bostanji all year round and she needs a reliable man with her. You won't even have to do any domestic duties or cooking, and she won't let you go short of pocket money. Well, what do you say?'

What could Thickhead say? Left to himself, he would never have gone off the ship at all, but the Lieutenant had set his heart on it and that was that. There was no help for it; he rapped out, 'Aye aye, sir!'

The Lieutenant's 'aunt' turned out to be a little woman in her early sixties, still using make-up on her face and mascara on her eyelashes, an absolute clown. She was called Güzide Hanim. She had a daughter of twenty-one or twenty-two, yellow-haired, rosy-cheeked, a Bosnian beauty. The girl's name was Nüvide or Nemide or something of that sort, but at home they called her Nonosh. Judging from what Thickhead said, Güzide Hanim was not really the Lieutenant's aunt. Nor, when you got down to it, was the Lieutenant really a lieutenant; in civilian life he was a champion swimmer, so he was now doing his reserve officer service in the Navy. From the fact that he had a photo of the girl hanging in his locker, it was obvious that he had fallen for Nonosh while he was a civilian and that his present aim was to get round her and ensnare her, with the help of his naval uniform. The moment he passed out as a new-fledged officer, he must have told them, 'I shall find an orderly for you.' After all, he wasn't an employment agency; that's just the way bad officers behave.

Nevertheless, Thickhead didn't have much to complain about. 'The day I went there,' he said, 'they made such a fuss of me! They couldn't do enough for me. I was surprised. Later I even felt quite ashamed. You see this suit? It belonged to her late husband. The shirt and the tie are presents from the Lieutenant, and the rosette came from the chauffeur. There's damn-all work. Now and then I have to get some odds and ends from the grocer, and that's about it.'

When he came the following week, he was distinctly worried. 'Things have got complicated,' he said. 'This Sunday the Lieutenant came to dinner at the villa. First of all he buttered me up a bit. Then he took me on one side and came clean. Do you know why he brought me here? Seems this Güzide Hanim has got a nephew who's a right pest. To start with, he fell for the girl in a big way, but they wouldn't let her marry him. Then there's some funny business about a legacy. They inherited a packet; I don't know if they've done him out of his share, or what. In fact it's a right mess. He's been threatening them, "I'm not going to leave her here with you, I'll do for the pair of you." Now you see why they made such a fuss of me. I was supposed to be going to protect them from that creep.' He took from his pocket a sparkling new Walther. 'The Lieutenant gave me this as well,' he said. 'Nine millimeter, but it's not the one they make at Kirikkale, the sort the military police use. A genuine Walther, this is. Made in Germany.'

I shall never forget. It was the watermelon season. We took an unripe one and set it up ten paces away, then we had some target practice. I hit it once in three shots. Thickhead didn't manage to hit it at all. 'They've found the right chap to be a bodyguard,' I said. 'Anyone who relies on you needs his head examined.' But as soon as the words were out of my mouth I realized I had made a mistake. Even though he did his best not to show it, it was clear that the boy was scared stiff. It was all that cursed machismo; he had accepted a responsibility and now there was no turning back. Where was the sense in breaking his morale?

When he came to see us the following week, he was smiling. 'Shall I tell you something, guv'nor?' he said. 'It was all a lot of bull. You'll see. For one thing, a man doesn't show off about going to kill someone; if he's got any guts he'll come and do it. The way I look at it, the fellow's idea is to squeeze money out of them.'

'You can't be sure of that,' I said. 'You be careful.'

So fond was Güzide Hanim of gadding about, and so addicted was she to her pleasures and amusements, that in spite of the threats she never once gave up going anywhere she meant to go. Today Chamlija, tomorrow Göksu, next day Hünkiar, the day after that I don't know where. She had the chauffeur with her, and Thickhead with his loaded pistol, so she wasn't worried.

After a week had passed without incident, Thickhead was becoming a real tough guy. When he came to see us at the fourth weekend, he was so bouncy that we didn't recognize him. His head was pulled down between his shoulders, he walked in a peculiar way, reminiscent of Humphrey Bogart, and every few minutes he would draw his pistol and twirl it nonchalantly on one finger. The boy had become the complete private eye.

At that time I was sent to Hatay on business and was therefore unable to follow the course of events.

I got back on a Friday, and Friday was Thickhead's day off, but there was no sign of him. I went up to the café and asked. They stared at me. 'Didn't you see it in the papers?'

'See what?'

'Thickhead's been wounded.'

'I don't believe it.'

'As true as I'm standing here, he's in the Naval Hospital at Kasimpasha.'

130

And, true enough, there he was, lying in bed, weak as a kitten, his arm and neck bandaged. His face had shrunk, and his complexion was yellowish green.

'How did it happen?' I asked.

In a broken voice, out of breath by the end of each sentence, he told me.

The previous Sunday they were on the way home from Büyükdere. How can one guess what is going to happen? They always came back via Maslak, but that day they felt like taking the lower road. 'Just as we got to Kurucheshme,' he said, 'we ran out of petrol. We stopped at a petrol station and a grey Dodge came along and braked right in front of us. A long-legged skinny bloke, like a lizard, got out and came straight for us. He opened the back door of our car. I was staring like an idiot, wondering what he was up to. The moment he opened the door, he fired his gun. The slimy, filthy, rotten bastard!'

The first shot sent Güzide Hanim's handbag flying in the air, the second grazed Nonosh's earlobe and shattered the window, the third – ah yes, the third. The third shot went straight and buried itself in the shoulder of our daft Thickhead, who was shielding them. Before the thug could fire a fourth shot, the chauffeur had grabbed his hand.

'It happened so suddenly,' said Thickhead, 'I couldn't make out what was going on. I saw he was still firing so I thought at least I'd put myself in front of the lady and protect her.'

'You really were a bloody fool,' I said. 'Was that your job, you clot? They've scores to settle between them. All right, you were caught napping and you couldn't make a move fast enough. Then let him shoot her and do her in, let him do whatever he feels like. Suppose you'd died for nothing! You have a mother; didn't you feel pity for her?'

'That's a terrible thing you've said, guv,' he said. 'I beg of you, don't talk like that. What have they been giving me my bread for? I did my duty. I've had a decent upbringing, guv.'

For fully three and a half months, in the Naval Hospital at Kasimpasha, Thickhead paid the penalty for having had a decent upbringing. At first, Güzide Hanim and Nonosh came frequently to visit their loyal and self-sacrificing Thickhead. Well, I say 'visit'; all they actually did on these visits was to say, 'How awful!' Once and only once they thought of bringing him some of his favourite flaky pastry. Then their visits became less and less frequent. Gradually they tailed off entirely. Once or twice they sent the chauffeur. After that, they even stopped asking after him. Güzide Hanim's nephew being in jail, there was no further need of a bodyguard. They gave him a total of three hundred liras and closed the account. All Thickhead got, or ever would get, from protecting Güzide Hanim was the good meals he ate during the three and a half months he spent in hospital, a couple of free trips in the car to the picnic-spots of Istanbul, and a crippled left arm which he could not turn the way he wanted and with which he could make only a few limited movements.

If his self-sacrifice had been good for anything, it had certainly done nothing for the Lieutenant. He failed to ingratiate himself with Güzide anyway. She had of course accepted his protection purely to escape the evil of her pestilential nephew. Once the danger from that quarter had been removed, she showed him the door. In fact, for quite some time Nonosh had been having an affair with the son of an olive-oil merchant from Ayvalik, who was at least as handsome as the Lieutenant. He reminded one faintly of Glen Ford. Moreover, he had a red Rolls-Royce and the latest model Criscraft, just like the ones at the Moda Yacht Club. And if it came down to uniforms, he had done his reserve officer service at the Heybeli Naval College. Eventually Nonosh went off to the son of the merchant from Ayvalik, and the Lieutenant was given the air. Standard procedure.

Six months before Thickhead was due for discharge he was invalided out on account of his arm, with no notion what to do next. With his disability, he could not work as a porter or bootblack, nor as a bus-conductor or boatman.

We had a whip-round and as he had no alternative he accepted the bit of money we collected and used it as capital, to set up as a seller of sweets, chewing-gum and sandwiches at the Dolmabahche Stadium.

I always say Istanbul is a small town, and no one believes me. But Istanbul really and truly is a small town. So one day, on the grandstand, I think it was at a Fener–Beshiktash match, Thickhead bumped into the Lieutenant whom Nonosh had jilted. Having by now been discharged, he was wearing a sports jacket, and had a camera slung round his neck. Sitting next to him was a pretty blonde, by no means inferior to Nonosh, and they were talking and laughing together in a very intimate fashion.

Now look at Thickhead's nobility of soul. 'You've been discharged, sir,' he says, 'good luck to you.' Not a word about 'This affliction of mine is because of you. Look, I'm crippled and can't get a job.' Just 'You've been discharged, sir, good luck to you.' That's all.

Still, it seems that the Lieutenant whom Nonosh had jilted was a sensible boy. He stood up and, with evident sincerity, threw his arms round Thickhead. 'So long as I'm there, Kiazim Efendi,' he said, 'you aren't done for yet.' Confronted with this gesture of humanity, Thickhead's eyes filled with tears and if he were not ashamed to do so he would have burst out crying on the spot. The Lieutenant's eyes too were wet. Who knows? Maybe it was because the sight of Thickhead had reminded him of Nonosh. When they had unclasped each other, the Lieutenant turned to his new betrothed and said, 'Darling, Kiazim Efendi here was my orderly when I was in the service. He would have died if I'd told him to. That's the kind of brave and loyal young man he is.'

Thereupon Darling and the Lieutenant looked at each other and had a whispered conversation. Then the Lieutenant took a visiting-card out of his pocket and wrote an address at the bottom.

Thickhead brought the card along to me. 'Goodness is not dead in the world, guv,' he said, and that was all he said. The place the Lieutenant had noted down on the card, by way of recommendation, was a biscuit factory at Kazlicheshme. Thickhead went there the next day. It turned out that the proprietor of the factory, which made Jeyhan brand extra-special biscuits, was none other than Darling's father, the Lieutenant's future father-in-law.

They gave Thickhead a job on the spot, as night-watch-man. A hundred and ten a month. What more could he want?

When he came and reported this, the chaps at the café teased him. 'You devil,' they said, 'you've struck lucky again.'

There are some people who only realize they are well off when someone else envies them. Our Thickhead was one such. He was particularly worried about the jealous gaze of Halil the carpenter. To avert the Evil Eye, he recited charms over himself and spat, and wherever he saw wood he would knock on it. He only stopped short of having himself fumigated by a sorceress.

But nothing he did was of any use. Before the month was out he turned up, utterly dejected. He put the blame on Halil. 'Those blue eyes of yours!' he said.

The cause of his dismissal was seemingly a fabrication. The foreman was a master craftsman when it came to pinching flour and sugar, but he had not been able to smuggle it out of the factory. He hid it but it was discovered and he accused Thickhead. But this wasn't the real reason. For one thing, even if they believed Thickhead, why should they sack the foreman? The boss realized that Thickhead was innocent; he realized that all right but as this was the time when the Lieutenant fell out with the boss's daughter and left her, he took it out on the Lieutenant's man. Being somebody's man can sometimes have evil consequences, you see. So there was poor old Thickhead, all crestfallen, with twenty-three liras in his pocket. The season was over, there weren't even any league matches at which he might hope to run into the Lieutenant on the grandstand. Even if he did, the Lieutenant was a poor thing who could do with some influence himself. It was not likely that he would have secured some other manufacturer's daughter.

Having given up hope of his protector, Thickhead was obliged to look out for himself.

During the years which I spent away from Istanbul, I

heard he had gone on to the freighters on the Mediterranean run, and was constantly coming and going between Haifa, Egypt and Tunis. Then, as usual, he lost his job, because he was made the scapegoat in a smuggling conspiracy in which he was in no way involved. 'So help me God,' he said, and I believe him. Later he worked in Haydarpasha railway station, the Kadiköy vegetable market and for a while, despite his crippled arm, in the fire brigade, thanks to the patronage of the then Sub-Governor.

By the time I came home he was unemployed again. The Director was reducing staff, and Thickhead, as a cripple, was the first to be sacked. As his mother could no longer go out to do people's washing as she used to do, they were in dire straits.

Among his acquaintances there was a retired inspector of schools, God bless him, a respected and influential man who begged and pleaded and got Thickhead a job as stores assistant at a secondary school, at ninety liras a month, and this saved the boy from destitution.

Once he'd found a job there was no holding him.

He turned up suddenly one morning and said, 'Guv'nor, I be getting married.' Though he was an Istanbul man through and through, he talked in that countrified fashion at times when he was very pleased about something or felt a bit above himself. If only there were something to make him feel like that, poor devil!

'Congratulations!' I said. 'Who's the lucky girl?'

He smiled in embarrassment and looked straight ahead of him. 'Nakibe Hanim, the wife of the chap from the café, found her,' he said. He was still looking straight ahead, intently picking at a fleck of whitewash that had stuck to the wall, as though it was the only job in all the world that he had to do.

'What kind of a girl is she?'

'I haven't seen her yet. She saw me (he blushed) and liked the look of me (he was clearly having difficulty in suppressing a smirk). I hear she's a cheerful sort, quiet. She's been brought up in a very posh house. The lady she works for is the wife of Ali Riza Bey. He's a Member of Parliament.

135

You'll know him. They live at Ajibadem. She's a fosterling but they don't treat her any different from their own.'

'Do they know how much you make a month?'

'Nakibe Hanım's told them. She says the girl said, "I'm not looking for money, I'm satisfied with a crust. What matters is that the one who's going to be my husband should be a man and not leave me beholden to people I can't do with."'

'Good girl! Will you take her to live at your mother's?'

'Oh no! I'm going to buy an apartment, ain't I? Are you trying to be funny, guv?'

'All right, but what if the girl wants a home of her own? You'll have to come to an understanding about that.'

'That's easy. My mum is her mum too. But we haven't met face to face yet. They don't even let her out in the street.'

'You mean girls are still being kept out of sight of men in this day and age?'

'Maybe they are and maybe they aren't, but being as how these people are following the old ways, my mum will go and see her tomorrow. If she likes the look of her, I'm willing.'

I realized that Thickhead was ready to take any one, whoever she might be. So long as she liked the look of him, as he put it. For the first time in his life, here was a woman who genuinely liked him, believed in him, was ready to share her life with him. To be liked by a woman. He might be ugly, a pauper, a freak; never mind. To be liked. Do you realize what a big word that is, gentlemen? Thickhead was still looking straight ahead, trying not to show his joy and thinking he was succeeding, but it was obvious that he was bubbling over with delight. Nor could he be blamed. Which of us is any different? All it takes is a few words of commendation from a female throat in the morning, and there's no holding us. Great oxen that we are, all day long we are pleased with ourselves, with the world, with the human race. A few words, that's enough. That's how the Trojan War started. That's the cause of all wars. All crimes are committed because of that. If the cost of living is high, that's the reason. That's the reason for the black market. The contractor uses crumbling bricks, the official embezzles, the journalists quarrel, Ahmet rows with Mehmet, Ali throws Veli out of his job, the elder brother throws his younger brother out of the house; that is what motivates all of them.

'Good luck to you, Thickhead,' I said. 'I hope you'll be happy.'

'Thanks, guv,' he replied. 'I hope your turn comes soon.'

That week his mother went to see the girl, and liked the look of her. True, she was a tiny bit older than Thickhead, but, as his mother said, 'She's fine. She's quick and tidy, not afraid of work, and not so ugly that you can't bear to look at her face.'

At the wish of the people of the quarter, the girl's side agreed to hold the engagement party in Feyzullah's café. Huriser's mistress – Huriser was the girl's name – was rich and all that, but not stuck-up. For the girl's sake, the whole lot came to the party. Thickhead was in the seventh heaven, and he won everybody's affection. In honour of the betrothal, Shaban the butcher got up and did a *zeybek*, one of the wild folk-dances of the south-west. Shaban, a man who had never been known to dance at his own sons' circumcision feast! The headmaster, the superintendent of police, Nejmi Bey who owned the factory, all the tradesmen and all the hawkers; there were no absentees.

Huriser's mistress gave the newly-engaged couple permission to meet and go out together once a week. It was summertime, you know. The first week, Thickhead took his betrothed to the Istanbul Exhibition. The second week, they went to the Gülhane Park. They sat on one of the benches overlooking the sea and ate pumpkin-seeds and roast chick-peas. From there, Thickhead suggested that they should go to the Marmara Cinema, to which Huriser agreed. But when Thickhead was about to take a box, she became suspicious. She was on the point of leaving him there and walking by herself to the tram. He wore himself out calming her down. What he told me – and I don't know if it was the truth or if he was lying – was this: 'I did it to test her. If she had come with me to a box, believe me, she'd have gone down in my esteem. She's not a woman, guv, she's pure

137

gold; she's honour incarnate. She's a proper smasher.'

The story from now on is rather like something out of the cinema, but that is not my fault. Sometimes events in real life can be far more dramatic than any scenario dreamed up by our native film industry.

I didn't see the fire myself, but I heard about it from those who did. Lame Aziz told me about it, and then I had it from Thickhead. The residents of the Ajibadem quarter said the first sign was at midnight, when the windows started to crack. Everyone looked and saw that Huriser's mistress's house was on fire. Lame Aziz reckoned that the owners did it to collect the insurance, but according to the neighbours it was entirely accidental. The master and mistress were at the club that night, gambling. As it was a Friday, the washing had been done that day, and apparently the laundrywoman had not made sure the furnace was out before she left. The furnace burned on unnoticed and the fire caught the dry kindling stacked beside it. It was midnight and nobody knew. Anyway, the house was an old building and it was like tinder; in an instant it was enveloped in flames.

Well, what's important isn't the fire but the consequences of the fire. If there's a fire at Ajibadem, you don't expect the lads of Yeldeghirmen, Ibraamagha, and Misirlioghlu to stay put, do you? People came swarming in from all directions, and among them, of course, was Thickhead. For one thing, his betrothed lived in Ajibadem. And besides, as you know, he had been a fireman in his time. The scene was like Judgment Day. The fire-fighting crews had not been late in arriving, but the fire had spread very rapidly. There were bells, sirens, men shouting and calling to each other in the night, multitudinous flames like devils' tongues licking at the darkness, venerable walls crackling as they caught alight, then breaking away and falling in ruin. The family got out straight away. They thought of Huriser some time later.

The girl had a name for being so sound a sleeper that a cannon fired by her head would not waken her. When it all began she must have been dead to the world, and now she was imprisoned inside. She was done for; she was going to be burned alive. Thickhead was not going to stand looking on while his darling, his only one, was perishing in there amidst the flames. He broke through the cordon and made a dash for the house, ignoring the cries of 'Don't! Don't! It's going to collapse any second!' I can just picture Thickhead, pushing the police out of his way and courageously advancing towards the house with those crab-like legs of his. He charged straight at the stairs and, struggling against the stifling smoke, hurled himself into the first-floor hall. From one of the rooms there came the crying of a child. 'Mummy, Mummy, please wake up, Mummy! The house is on fire!'

Thickhead kicked the door in and plunged inside. What met his eyes was Huriser, sound asleep. Beside her, pulling at her, was a three-year-old girl. So astonished was he at the sight of the mother and daughter that he quite forgot about the fire. What saved him was the chief fire officer shouting from outside, 'The stairs have collapsed! Quick, jump out of the window!' He collected his wits. The firemen, most of them friends of his, had stretched out a tarpaulin and were waiting. First he tossed the little girl out. After her he threw Huriser, still totally oblivious. Finally he jumped out himself. Down below there was applause, joy, commotion. The young people and the children were deliriously cheering the hero of the hour.

Huriser's mistress was overjoyed to see her and her daughter, of whose lives she had despaired. She did not even notice that their lies had been exposed. But Thickhead's face was like a thunder-cloud. He broke through the throng and was lost in the darkness.

When I saw him next day he was adamant. 'I'm not marrying her.' He had a bottle of raki in front of him; he was drinking and darkly brooding. 'It's right what they say, you can't make firewood from a lime tree or a wife from a fosterling.' For her part, Huriser sent word to say, 'He doesn't have to be afraid. I shan't make him pay for the child's keep. I get an allowance for her from her father. If that doesn't work out, I shall send her to my mother.' Poor Huriser was so fed up with not having a home of her own that she would gladly live in poverty. But Thickhead was obdurate. She had lied to him, hadn't she? What angered him

139

far more than the possibility of having to pay for the daughter's keep was that he had been deceived, made a fool of, tricked into believing that Huriser, who had had two husbands (there perhaps he was exaggerating), was a virgin. He had nothing to reproach himself for; if there was one thing he could not stand it was lying and hypocrisy.

In short the engagement was broken off. And with it was broken Thickhead's morale, even his health. It was a tragic situation.

The other day he came over to me under the plane tree, and sat down. 'You can say what you like,' he said, 'it's no good. They call me Thickhead and that's exactly what I am. I'm Thickhead and that's it; what else?'

'No,' I said, 'you mustn't talk like that.'

He tugged at his nose. 'Is it a lie, guv? I mean, is it a lie? Everything I've ever set my hand to has gone wrong.'

He was unshaven, and the collar of his greasy jacket was badly worn. His right hand was bandaged, so he was trying to light a cigarette with his crippled hand. He couldn't manage it, and dropped both match and cigarette.

I was sorry for the boy. But then I was angry with myself. Whenever we feel sorry for someone, is there not latent in that feeling, whether we admit it or not, a rather foolish pride in our own superiority?

'Get your head up, Thickhead. It doesn't suit you to cry like a woman.'

He raised his head, but went on tugging at his nose.

I said, 'If you are Thickhead, so what? Are you the only Thickhead in the whole world? Never mind that I go around a little tidier than you, that I shave every day, wear a shirt that's been ironed, and carefully comb back the two hairs I have in front so as to hide my bald patch. Leave aside the outward appearance and there's no great difference between us, my dear Thickhead. No, don't make polite noises, this is a fact. I am no less of a thickhead than you. If anything, your thickheadedness is written in small letters and mine perhaps in capitals. Believe me, that's the only difference.'

He raised his eyebrows and looked to see if I was joking. 'Why do you say you're a thickhead, guv?' he asked. 'Why do you reckon you're like me? After all, you're a gent.'

'Shut up and listen,' I replied. 'You were wounded when, like a fool, you put yourself in the way of the bullets that were aimed at Güzide Hanim and Nonosh. I'm so stupid that although I wasn't a paid bodyguard like you and didn't make my living at it, I put myself in the way of bullets of a different kind that were aimed at people I thought were my friends. And I was wounded in a different way from you, but more seriously. Is that a lie?'

'It's the truth,' he said. He bowed his head, upset on my account. Bless him, he's very soft-hearted.

'Next, in order to discover that the girl you loved had a child, to catch her out in her lying, you had to get into a burning house and fight the flames, just like in the American films. Whereas I very quickly detected my loved one's lies and the fact that she was two-faced – indeed four- or five- or eight- or ten-faced – while I was in bed or at the tea-table.'

'God damn all women,' said Thickhead.

'So you see that we are two of a kind, from whatever angle you examine our lives,' I said. 'You put your trust in the Lieutenant and got into the biscuit factory, and look how they sacked you. I got into many biscuit factories without being anybody's man, and when they sacked me they didn't even think it necessary to cook up reasons.'

We both sighed.

It was getting near midday. A bean-scented breeze came out of the neighbouring houses, and licked our faces as it passed. Thickhead was deep in thought.

'Do you remember,' I said, 'the times you played for Thunderbolt Sport?'

He suddenly came to life. 'Will I ever forget? What about the time we drew two-all with Vefa B? And once we beat Anadoluhisar four–nil on their own ground.'

'Correct,' I said. 'What position were you playing then?'

'Right-half.'

'And me?'

'Left-half.'

'That means there was a resemblance between us as long ago as that. What are you now?'

141

'A lousy storeman.'

'And me?' He didn't answer, so I went on, 'Me, I'm a lousy apology for a schoolmaster.' Cutting short his polite protestations, I said, 'That means, Thickhead Efendi my brother, that since those days we have both continued to be half-backs. Sometimes other people have scored the goals and got the credit. It looks as though we shall go on being half-backs, and other people will go on scoring the goals. Being half-backs is our destiny; what else is there to say?'

Thickhead put his crippled arm on my shoulder and gave me a look of mingled affection and pity. 'Never mind, guv. The most important thing is good health.'

After that, we both sat down and had some tripe-soup.

The curious thing is that what I had said to him, just to take his mind off his troubles, had got to me, and I cannot tell you how much it hurt.

Thickhead had voided the bitterness inside him, and had found in me one who shared his destiny. Shortly afterwards he went off, happy in that feeling of superiority which comes of being able to pity someone other than oneself. He was holding a cornel-wood stick, with which he swished cheerfully at the laurels as he went.

I stayed there alone, my head in my hands, thinking.

No Trouble At All

[Some of the author's former colleagues at Istanbul University still delight in identifying the originals of the characters in this story, which was written in 1965. The Junta, to which frequent reference is made, was the group of officers who overthrew the government of Adnan Menderes in May 1960. In October they dismissed 147 university teachers, but were subsequently obliged by public opinion to reinstate them.]

Sedat Germiyanoghlu parked his 1963 Chevrolet, which he had brought back with him from his Fulbright Fellowship, next to the coal heaps. He took off his chamois leather gloves and locked up. Quickly, because it was raining, he crossed the courtyard and went into the Faculty building.

On Mondays he had two classes one after the other, so on Tuesdays he generally felt a little frail. On top of that, on this particular Tuesday he had drunk rather a lot at the Rotary Club luncheon. His plan for the afternoon had been to take a bit of a nap, have a cool shower and meet Mr Pritchett in the bar of the Park Hotel. Before he could do any of these things, the blasted telephone had rung. For this reason, whoever the candidate might be, he could at that moment have voted against him with no trouble at all.

As he got out of the lift at the third floor, Ragip Avshar came dashing to meet him. It was pretty obvious that he'd been waiting for him, listening out for the noise of the lift.

'Thank heaven you've come, Professor,' he said. 'I was so scared I mightn't be able to get hold of you. I'm counting on you.'

'Wasn't your promotion to professor debated at the last Council meeting?'

'They didn't have a quorum.'

'If they didn't have a quorum, how did Nejati's promotion get turned down?'

'Being a senior lecturer, I was there while they were discussing his application. But I went out when they started

143

talking about my application. That left them one short of the quorum.'

'If only Nejati had gone in then!'

'Nejati can't attend Council; he's not a senior lecturer.'

Although he tried to hide it, there was a stealthy joy in Ragip Avshar's tone of voice. It was perfectly obvious that he'd voted against Nejati at last week's meeting so as to keep the vacancy open for himself. Sedat Germiyanoghlu looked at this candidate for a professorship who was standing before him. This lumpish young man, who habitually wore three-buttoned jackets with vents at the back and also went in for stringy bow-ties, today, like every lecturer whose promotion was under discussion, was casually dressed, just for the hell of it. As he spoke he clasped his two plump hands in front of him and shook his head from side to side. But however inoffensive and wronged he might try to look, with his bulk he couldn't manage it.

Sedat Germiyanoghlu was downright upset that Nejati, who had lost his chance last week, was of too lowly an academic rank to attend Council meetings; could not cast an opposing vote today, when this man's promotion was being debated. No, not just because they hadn't had a quorum and had disturbed him. Fair's fair; it wasn't merely for that. It was a bit because the sense of equity, that in spite of everything still lay curled up and sleeping inside him, desired this redressing of the balance. At that moment, Sakip Özbashar came out of the committee room and at great speed walked into Sabahat Hanim's room.

'You see?' said Ragip Avshar. 'They're not wasting time. Ihsan jumped into Sebati's car a moment ago and went off to round people up. They're even going to get Ayetullah Bey out of his sickbed and bring him.'

'What's the matter with Ayetullah Bey?'

'You know, he's had a hernia operation.'

Ragip didn't like the way the conversation had been side-tracked from his own fight for promotion to Ayetullah Bey's hernia operation. 'In short,' he said, 'they're determined to sabotage me.'

Sedat pondered. Who are 'they'? Why are they rounding

people up? Given that they mean to sabotage him, why are they trying to get a quorum, instead of simply staying away from the meeting and letting it be cancelled? And just what the hell kind of a chap is this Ragip? What has he done to deserve to be made a Professor of Ethnography? And how did he get to be so chummy with me that he can confidently say, 'I'm counting on you'? And have the cheek to phone me at home, out of the blue, when it looks as if there may not be a quorum? Work that out, if you can.

Sabahat Hanim's door was open, and Sakip Özbashar's voice was coming out of it:' 'Hallo! Sakip speaking. Forgive me for bothering you, Professor. I believe Jevat has spoken to you. I understand you promised to be at the meeting today . . . Oh no, Professor! Jevat doesn't think we should boycott the meeting so as to get it called off. He says if we do they'll only bring the matter up at the next meeting; we should get it over with today. That's right, Professor. That's the man. We're counting on you, Professor. We're expecting you.'

Ragip had turned pale. Clearly the hope that they would boycott the meeting had been his last card. Now that that had gone, he lapsed into a state of imbecility; that pretentious, donnish attitude of his flew away and he was suddenly as bewildered as a Kastamonu herdsman who's just been sacked from the farm.

Sedat looked in the direction of Sabahat Hanim's room. He fancied that he detected a crafty piece of tactics in the way in which it had been arranged for that telephone conversation, which could perfectly well have been carried on behind closed doors and in a low voice, to be audible from where they stood. In their parliamentary tricks, these people had lately outdone even the political wolves. If they were Members of Parliament themselves, what wouldn't they be capable of! But he immediately saw that, even if they were Members of Parliament, they could never pull off a stroke like this. He felt sorry for Ragip Avshar. At that moment he could, with no trouble at all, have voted for this poor victim who was being so cunningly nobbled in the race for promotion.

Imadettin Bey, the Professor of Islamic History, who was coming out of the men's room, had opened his sheet-sized handkerchief and was drying his hands. Anyone could have taken him for a Land Registry official who had just performed his ablutions at the fountain of the New Mosque and was getting ready to pray.

A faint glimmer of hope dawned on Ragip Avshar's face. 'Praise be!' he said. 'He's on our side.'

In his voice there was the warmth of thankfulness. In his eyes there was pride, a pride which meant, 'You people are supporting me, aren't you? Though I may not win, one who is vanquished in this cause can be counted as victorious. The honour of this is sufficient for me.'

It was not very agreeable for Sedat Germiyanoghlu to find himself ranked alongside Imadettin Bey. What kind of cause might rally him, who was reckoned to be the most Western and, according to his enemies, the most snobbish professor in the Faculty, under the same flag as Imadettin Bey, the most obstinately Oriental and Ottoman of the teachers? Possibly the Erzinjan earthquake. Possibly the Cyprus question. But the very dicey promotion of a shifty lecturer? Right from the start he had never been able to get on good terms with this pockmarked Professor of Islamic History; maybe because he reminded him of his grandfather, who had been the sexton of a mosque and whom he was for ever trying to forget and to make others forget. Whenever he was obliged to mention Imadettin Bey he referred to him as 'the usher'. At every opportunity, he underlined the differences of training, style and mentality between them, in veiled remarks which he termed 'second-degree witticisms', which Imadettin Bey could not easily comprehend and whose flavour could be appreciated only by such members of Council as had had a British or American education. Imadettin Bey used to respond to these remarks with some coarse lines of classical poetry or resounding quatrains from the satirist Neyzen, murmured in a voice loud enough to be heard only by the Professors of Persian Literature and of Classical Ottoman Literature, who sat beside him. Certainly none of this could be considered likely to reduce the tension between the two. No, being on the same side as Imadettin Bey could, apart from anything else it might do, deal a very nasty blow to the prestige of his witticisms in future.

He glanced at the young man, who in the meantime had largely pulled himself together, had stopped looking like a wretched and hapless herdsman and now looked like a sullen ex-captain of gendarmerie. Now, for this reason alone, he could with no trouble at all have voted against him.

Sakip Özbashar must have talked Sabahat Hanim round, for he went with her into the committee room, rubbing his hands. Sabahat Hanim had an air of being perpetually cross with somebody. You know there are people who can't do without a grudge, who can go on only if they're at daggers drawn with someone, whose lives are empty otherwise? Well, she was one of those.

When Sedat Germiyanoghlu approached the door, the Council messenger rose from his stool. As the door, much like that of any low dive, was in constant use, the poor man was doomed never to have a proper sit-down. As Sedat went in, Ragip whispered, 'Stand firm, Professor! I'm counting on you.'

A warm cloud of cigarette-smoke licked Sedat Germiyan-oghlu's face. Since the smoke was combined with steam from the defective radiator, the visibility inside was zero. Making his way forward like an infantryman taking up position in a smoke-screen laid by the tanks, he perched on a vacant chair next to Müshtak Ulash.

Ziya Boztepe was reading the selection committee's report. The monotony of his voice, reminiscent of a Justices' Clerk, lent the report he was reading the gravity of the verdict at a criminal trial. Müshtak Ulash put his colleague in the picture: 'We're on the question of the Chair of Anthropology. The committee are divided four to one. Rüknettin Atamer voted against, and his dissenting opinion is going to be presented separately.'

Sedat Germiyanoghlu picked up the agenda; it was only then that he realized that Ragip Avshar, whom for some reason he'd got fixed in his head as Lecturer in Ethnography, was in fact Lecturer in Anthropology. Next he gave a yawn.

147

He picked up the well-sharpened pencil in front of him. He started to scribble importantly on the snow-white paper that also lay there. Any outside observer might have thought he had noticed a flaw in Article Three of the committee's report. What he was in fact doing was drawing a battleship. Ever since he was a boy, his speciality had been to draw battleships dashing the sea into foam. Much as naval architecture might have progressed since the Second World War, there was no change in the lines of his dreadnoughts, all of which looked like the *Yavuz*, the pride of the Ottoman Navy in World War One.

Since his head worked better when he was shading in his drawings, he now began to make an assessment of the situation. He at once grasped the connection between Sakip Özbashar's telephone call on behalf of Jevat's lot, and Rüknettin Atamer's desire to present his adverse opinion in a separate report. If the supporters of the Junta vote against the candidate, then the people the Junta tried to get rid of will vote for him. If they do, Nihat's group of independents will support them. Let's suppose that, of that group, Hilmi and Ilhami support Jevat's lot. But Idris will swerve to the other side, sure as eggs is eggs. As the German members of the Faculty always take their cue from him, that makes seven more votes from there and that adds up to what? Twenty-eight. Now Ragip, snivelling outside; if the thing's sewn up that tight, why is he carrying on as if he was a victim of intrigue? Is it because he's a fool or is it because he's a crafty barrack-room lawyer? So long as it really is in the bag, what I'll do now is, towards the end of the discussion I'll take the floor and deliver an oration. I'll bring in the facts that the candidate is unworthy of the Chair of Ethnography – sorry, Languages of Hither Asia or whatever the hell it is, that professorships have recently been dished out to all and sundry with very doubtful justification and that this is scarcely conducive to enhancing the prestige of the Faculty, which is low enough as it is. Then I'll sit down. This won't prevent Ragip Avshar from getting his promotion when it comes to the vote and at the same time it will demonstrate yet again my high-minded attitude, which is to defend excellence and only excellence, everywhere and at every time, and to prize the Faculty's European standards above all else.

It was at that precise moment that there came to his nostrils the scent of a European cigar. Sadi Tümay, his elbows planted on the table, sprawling like a camel, oblivious of everything, was totally engaged in smoking a cigar. Attaining to the awareness that he was smoking a cigar, extracting the full pleasure of it, he was contemplating the smoke. Sedat Germiyanoghlu consoled himself with the thought that it was only a King Edward. As if divining what was going through his mind, Said Tümay took the metal tube of the cigar out of his pocket and rolled it across the green baize tablecloth. Damn him! It was a Walter Upmann.

'Been robbing a bank, Sadi?'

Sadi didn't say anything. He merely gave a gracious smile.

This fellow Sadi devoted all his energies to procuring invitations to the cocktail parties, luncheons and dinners of every foreign consulate in Istanbul. Once there, he never budged from in front of the buffet, eating steadily and drawing a bead with his eye on what he had not yet got round to eating. On one such occasion, Sedat himself had seen him smoke three cigars one after another and then, with complete assurance, deposit four more in his top pocket, as if he were loading ammunition into a bandolier. Say the fellow took, on average, three cigars at each official function, that meant he was stocked up for a month. And then, as was happening now, having got up from his two-and-a-half-lira canteen lunch of braised lamb, cold bean salad and stewed quince, he would extract one from his pocket or from its tube, breathe onto both sides of it, light it and amid the smoke be, for half an hour, a European. Sedat Germiyanoghlu had particularly noticed that Sadi always chose these cigar interludes as the time for reading his *Le Monde*.

Ziya Sungur had irritably taken the floor and was irritably speaking: 'I am not prying into the candidate's private life. I confine myself to drawing attention to one aspect of his conduct. If there are any among you who regard it as normal for a pure scholar to involve himself in party and electioneering intrigues and to give that involvement priority over the research activity of his own department, I would have them know that I do not share their point of view.'

Sedat Germiyanoghlu left the mast of the battleship half-done. He looked up and his eye fell on Niyazi Turanli. Niyazi Turanli, who was one of the group supporting the Junta, was listening intently to what was being said. He was obviously waiting for the end of the speech and wondering, 'Is this fellow getting at Avshar, or is he hinting at the fact that I'm a director of the Tourism Bank?'

Sakip Özbashar interrupted the speaker: 'Stop beating about the bush and come out with what you have to say.'

The Dean rapped on the table with his chubby hand. 'Let's not have any crosstalk,' he said. He himself didn't seem to have much confidence that with so small a noise he could recover his nonexistent authority.

Ziya Sungur said, 'I should like to say a brief word. This lecturer, who has come up before you as a candidate for a professorship, appeared in one of the parties' lists at the recent election as a candidate for Parliament. What more evidence do you need to show how self-seeking a man he is?'

Müshtak Ulash had the floor: 'What do you mean? I mean to say, why should a scholar deny himself a right, a – a – an honour (he sought for a more powerful word and couldn't find one), yes, an honour which is given to every citizen? If the last speaker will be kind enough to explain I shall be very grateful.' He sat down.

Ziya Sungur was not kind enough, so Dündar Sülünoghlu spoke. 'My dear colleagues,' he said, 'We are talking here within these four walls. I shall say no more than this: On this matter I am entirely with my friend Ziya Sungur, who sees the candidate as self-seeking. There are four of them, brothers, down in Mardin. The father is an Alaouite sheikh. They own eight villages and countless farms. At the last election, all four of them stood as candidates, each one for a different party. The idea was, whichever party won the election, there'd be a spokesman in Parliament to protect their joint family interests.'

'Excellent tactics!' said Sebati Yurdaer.

Dündar Sülünoghlu continued: 'I find it superfluous to

add anything. Thank you.' He sat down.

Sedat Germiyanoghlu hoisted a battle-flag on the mast of his dreadnought. He even made one of the gun-turrets open fire. Then, with great care, he began to shade in the smoke.

Ziya Sungur had risen to his feet and was shouting, 'Which party was he a candidate for? Which party?'

'Is that of any importance?'

'If you will allow me, yes it is. Suppose it was the Workers' Party?'

'And what if it were?'

'Please, my dear colleagues! We are not here to conduct an ideological debate.'

'In that case, come on! Let's have some propaganda for Kurdish separatism!'

There was a general laugh. Everyone knew that Ragip Avshar, like Müshtak Ulash, was a Kurd. The only one present who did not know it was the Dean, and because he didn't see the joke he took the laughter for some kind of impertinence. Consequently, when Müshtak Ulash leaped to his feet, saying, 'I have been the victim of a personal attack. I demand to speak,' he replied, 'There has been no personal attack. You may not speak.'

'There has!'

'There has not!'

Sadi Tümay decided to detach himself from his cigar for the duration of two sentences 'Let me reassure you. It was not the Workers' Party.'

Ragip Avshar's supporters breathed easier. Sadi Tümay continued: 'Nor was it the New Turkey Party.'

'What's this?' asked Sedat Germiyanoghlu. 'A *reductio ad absurdum*?'

As this witticism was not particularly second-degree, it made most people laugh. Sadi Tümay said, with a rising intonation like a town-crier, 'Nor was it the Justice Party!'

'What's left?' said Sakip Özbashar. 'The Republican People's Party.'

Sadi Tümay turned towards him and said, 'Yes, my dear colleagues. He was a Republican People's Party candidate.'

151

Haldun Taner

As if being a candidate for any other party was high treason, and as if he was a wily barrister who had saved his client from all these aspersions one after another, he had left his strongest trump till last. 'Yes, my dear colleagues,' he repeated. 'If you consider that being selected as RPP candidate for Mardin constitutes a disqualification, then go ahead, turn him down.' He was about to add, 'If you've got the guts', but he restrained himself and went back to his cigar.

In the 1964 elections, Sedat Germiyanoghlu, unable to withstand the insistence of his friends, had applied to be the RPP candidate for the Senate, for the Chanakkale constituency, but had been defeated in the selection process by a foreman porter. He suddenly felt an inward fury at Ragip Avshar who had passed the selection barrier at Mardin. 'The fellow has a finger in every pie,' he said to himself. 'Just look; he's even got allies among the Kurdish separatists. Rightists, leftists, Sunnites, Shiites, atheists, racists, westernizers, orientalizers; he knows how to get on with all of them. The fellow's a scoundrel.' As if turning like weathercocks were the exclusive prerogative of Istanbul folk, he added, 'The fellow's a crafty jumped-up peasant.'

If a vote had been taken at that moment, at least one vote could have been cast against Ragip Avshar with no trouble at all.

While these thoughts were going through his head, Rük- nettin Atamer had taken the floor and was reading his individual report which he had declared his intention of presenting separately from that of the committee: 'For one thing, the principal defect of the committee's report is that it has no statement of justification. A declaration that the candidate Ragip Avshar has completed his statutory period as a lecturer cannot be adduced as proof that he is worthy of a professorship. Standing orders specifically require, quite apart from this precondition, that the candidate's scholarly competence be made clear.'

'Well well!' murmured Sadi Tümay, 'Is he going to be tripped up on a technicality? You might as well have objected that he forgot to put a revenue stamp on his letter of application.'

152

Niyazi Turanli, who was one of the pro-Junta group, said, 'Please, let's listen to Atamer's report.'

'Quiet, everybody!' chorused Jevat's team.

Pertev Jandan's sense of fair play overwhelmed him. On the point of rebellion, he said, 'In that case, why didn't you object to the previous candidate we discussed? There was no statement of justification in the report on him, either.'

Another chorus, this time from the pro-Junta group: 'No going back on a decision once taken!'

Now that he had the moral support of that group, Rüknettin Atamer continued to read out his report, which he held at the tip of his nose, heedless of the extraneous vocal refrains. As he was not yet accustomed to his dentures, he produced occasional whistling noises.

'Moreover, of the forty-one items he mentions in his list of publications, thirty-seven are offprints not exceeding sixteen or, at most, thirty-two pages in length. As we can hardly count as a work of scholarship the book containing the candidate's collected articles from the *Jumhuriyet* newspaper, that means we are left with three works. They are: *Before Starting Anthropology, Anthropology and the Natural Sciences* and *The Limits of Anthropology*. The very names of these books demonstrate that the candidate is still sniffing around on the outside of anthropology and cannot summon up the courage to get into it. Consequently I move that the proposal be rejected.'

This speech was marked by laughter and cries of 'Jolly good!' from the pro-Junta group, and punctuated by even more excited shouts of 'Bravo!' When it was over, Sedat Germiyanoghlu felt the need to stand up and say something favourable. But he did not stand up. He could not speak. He had never suffered any harm from keeping quiet and waiting.

Shefkati Oghuztürk said, 'If sixteen-page offprints are not going to be shown as published works, I fear that most of our lists of publications will be pretty thin. Let's be honest, my friends. To be so hypercritical strikes me as an excess of zeal. What's fair for one is fair for all.'

'Hear hear!'

153

'In this very room,' Shefkati Oghuztürk went on, 'we have, when need arose, even promoted lecturers without doctorates to be professors. Come now, don't make me speak ill of anyone.'

'What's that? What's that?' cried Nedim, one of Jevat's group.

Was it because he hadn't heard? No, it was because he was a crafty swine. Shefkati Oghuztürk did not understand his tactics, which were to make sure that if any had failed to hear it they would hear it the second time round. So he repeated his statement word for word, as though what he'd said had been something really special.

For Jevat, this was a chance in a thousand. Giving Shefkati no time to regret his words, he leapt straight in: 'This extraordinary view, belittling the professors who have no doctorate, we repudiate with loathing. I personally have two doctorates; in this matter I can speak objectively. But I would ask you to permit me to make the following point clear: drawing distinctions between those with and those without doctorates results from a mean-spirited way of looking at things. I am convinced that the professors who have no doctorates have brought at least as much honour to this institution as the professors with doctorates.'

It was only at that moment that Shefkati Oghuztürk realized that he had really put his foot in it. He went as red as a beetroot. His gaffe had immediately offended the eleven professors on his side who had no doctorates; it might well make them switch to the other side. On top of that, what about those professors on the other side who had no doctorates? It would bring down on him their mortal enmity. He tried to think of something to say to retrieve the situation, but his mind had gone completely blank.

Ziya Sungur murmured, as he poured some mineral water into his glass from the bottle in front of him, 'That, gentlemen, is what they call an own goal.'

Silence fell, a heavy, oppressive silence.

It was broken by Ali Riza Bey. 'I haven't got two doctorates, like Jevat Sakaoghlu. I haven't even got one. Consequently, it I were to deny that I was aggrieved by our friend

Shefkati Bey's reproach, you'd none of you believe me.'

Sedat Germiyanoghlu groaned inwardly, because this was Ali Riza Bey's regular practice. He'd keep on and on doing his act about being offended at something and that would be his excuse for missing the next seven or eight meetings. It made it very difficult to get a quorum on Council. Ali Riza continued his speech, stringing together verses from Nefi, Karajaoghlan, Muallim Naji and Eshref. Finally he came to his peroration: 'It's not such a wonderful thing to have a doctorate. I could write a doctoral thesis analyzing the influences of Scottish literature on nineteenth-century Irish literature from the English point of view. Rather than expose myself to public derision in that way, I regard not doing a doctorate as the lesser of two evils.'

He really had disposed of that matter neatly. Now everyone, friend and foe, was laughing.

'Please,' said the Dean, 'let us return to the matter in hand. You are on the third item of the agenda; I mean, I have to remind you that we are debating the question of Ragip Avshar's professorship.'

The messenger came in with the tea. Sedat Germiyanoghlu drew the last battleship. The picture, which commemorated the battle of Jutland, could be considered finished. The serving of the tea seemed to ease the tension somewhat. Cevat's lot, like a basketball team gathered round their coach at halftime, deciding on tactics, had put their heads together and were making some sort of decision. Shefkati meanwhile was going to first one, then another of the professors without doctorates who had taken offence at his recent words, and was trying to soften what he had said. Every time he blundered into fresh contradictions.

Sedat Germiyanoghlu was thoroughly bored. If only, he thought, a vote were to be taken straight away and the matter could finish here and now. Ragip Avshar's professorship was no longer of importance. Now any kind of vote could be given, for, against, or abstaining. He drew the agenda towards him and looked:

1. Candidacies of Nejati Giray, Ragip Avshar and Mazlum Inal for the vacant chair in the Department of Palaeontology.

2. Reduction of the library budget.
3. Increase in the budget of the Institute of Islamic Sciences.
4. A further year's extension of leave of absence for Prof. Memduh Gezgin, now in America.
5. Proposal for replacing the seats in the third-floor men's room.
6. Selection of Faculty delegate to the International Universities Congress, to be held at Lisbon in February.

This last item was written very indistinctly. Sedat wondered why the Dean wasn't going himself. Perhaps he had taken account of the advantages of being in Munich for the Carnival and preferred to attend the Archaeology Congress there. A trip to Portugal in the February vacation wouldn't be at all bad, you know. Jahit, an old schoolfriend, was in Lisbon at the moment, as Ambassador. When he went, he ought to go by sea, getting the full pleasure of the journey. His eyes suddenly seemed dazzled by the brilliant sunshine on the ship's deck. Any moment now he'd take his sunglasses out of his pocket. And you can't beat Portuguese wine. He pictured himself driving under the palms with Jahit in the Embassy car, pennant flying.

So lost was he in his vision that it was some time before he noticed that he had drawn the logo of the State Maritime Lines on one of the dreadnoughts engaged in the battle of Jutland. He wrote a large question mark at the end of the item about Faculty representation in Portugal and passed it to Sadi Tümay. Sadi Tümay, by way of answer, wrote a name: 'Idris'. Damn the bloody man! He took the paper and wrote, 'Who promised it to him?' Back came the answer in writing: 'Who do you think? The Junta boys.'

So that was why Idris was keeping his mouth shut today; it was so as not to risk annoying anyone. To Idris you had to add the seven German professors and that meant eight votes. He was furious with Idris, the German professors and the pro-Junta clique. He turned the Maritime Lines logo into a black pirate flag. He drew two crossbones on the white ground, with a skull on top. Now, just to get back at the Junta supporters, he could with no trouble at all have

156

delivered a two-hour speech in favour of Ragip Avshar, whom till that moment he had totally forgotten. 'I should have thought of that one,' he said to himself. 'That's one I should have thought of. The fellow's not a sociologist, he's a grantologist.'

The door opened. Ayetullah Bey, who had been dragged out of his bed to vote, came in, supported on Ihsan's arm. Ayetullah Bey was walking with difficulty. It may only have been a hernia but the operation had obviously shaken the poor man. His cheeks were sunken and his neck stood like a stalk in the middle of his collar. He looked like a gallant old sea-captain who had been roused from his sleep in order to save the sinking ship. He took Jevat's arm. Those who had not managed to get to the hospital thronged round him with excessive warmth, trying, by kissing him, to win absolution for their remissness. Ayetullah Bey's eyes grew moist. A seat was found for him and somebody sent for tea.

Sedat Germiyanoghlu looked at Ihsan, who had jumped into Sebati's car to bring the bedridden to vote. There could be no tangible reason for him to go to such lengths just to scupper Ragip Avshar's election. Ihsan was past praying for. Ever since boyhood, intrigue had been a habit with him. Or perhaps hobby was a better word. A kind of party game which he found entertaining. He didn't engage in it for personal advantage; it was simply that by now it had become an addiction.

Nedim Gürozan was on his feet, speaking: 'I'm going to tell you a little anecdote, from my own experience. You know we have a Municipal Orchestra, our ragbag of a Philharmonic, most of them dentists or vets or chemists or bank clerks, who by night turn into orchestral performers. The son of a friend of mine wanted to join it. He went for an audition and they turned him down. I had been at school with the conductor and I went to see him. "There are lots of fiddlers in your orchestra no better than this boy," I said. "True," he replied. "They all got in through drag. It is precisely for this reason that the orchestra is such a dead loss. Let me at least start filling the vacancies with decent players and improve things a bit."'

There was general laughter and Nedim Gürozan said, 'You all get the point. I shan't bother you any further.'

They had promised Ayetullah Bey that he would cast his vote immediately and be taken back to his soft bed in style, in a private car. Now it was plain to see that he was wearied and bored by the interminable speeches. They had stationed Nejmi next to him like a Gestapo guard, to make sure he didn't escape. If Nejmi had his way he would have clapped him into solitary confinement. Anxious at Ayetullah Bey's fidgeting, Ihsan hurried over to him and began to tell one of his off-colour stories: 'There's this chap undressing one night in the sleeping-car and he hears a woman's voice from the next compartment . . .' Ayetullah Bey was all ears. He appeared to have forgotten for a moment the painful site of his operation, his aching lower regions.

Before the laughter at Nedim's witty intervention had died away, Niyazi took the floor. 'I move,' he said, 'that the candidate be really and truly made a professor.' This surprising suggestion from the pro-Junta Niyazi aroused even those who were asleep. He continued: 'The prestige of our Faculty is at stake. Without having yet been elected to his Chair, our friend Ragip Avshar has already had visiting-cards printed with 'Prof.' on them. And he's described as Professor in the contract he's had drawn up with his new landlord. My brother-in-law lives in the flat downstairs, that's how I know. Further, he has introduced himself as Professor to his colleagues in universities abroad and likewise to the Ford Foundation, to which he is applying for a grant. If we fail to elect him, we shall be leaving him in an awkward and false position. I submit the case to the discretion of this honourable assembly.'

The last vestiges of seriousness in this honourable assembly were blown away in a gale of laughter.

Sedat Germiyanoghlu was very angry indeed at the way in which the idiotic Ragip Avshar had jumped the gun and ruined everything. For the last few minutes he had been preparing some scintillating sentences and was watching out for his chance to aim them, like so many slaps in the face, at the integrity of the other side. But to stand up and defend the young man who had laid himself open to such ridicule would be a waste of these precious words. Rather than do that, he would say nothing now and would present his well-turned phrases, suitably modified, on some other occasion.

The Dean took a vote. Ragip Avshar lost, by 17 to 28.

Ayetullah Bey got to his feet and began looking for Ihsan, who was going to take him home. They all stood up and were on the point of going out for a smoke, when somebody remembered: 'Hey, there was a third candidate mentioned in the agenda!'

'That's right! So there was.'

'Who was it?'

'Someone called Mazlum Inal.'

'Never heard of him.'

'Does anybody know him?'

The Junta supporters didn't know him. Nobody knew him. Then Shakir Baran said, 'He's a lecturer at Erzurum University.'

'One moment,' said the Dean. 'Before we go on to the next item, I am opening the discussion on the third candidate.'

'That's not on,' said one of those who felt like a break. But one or two others called out, 'Agreed!'

'What is being agreed to? Opening the discussion or making the third candidate a professor?'

'Both! Both!'

'I am opening the discussion,' said the Dean. 'Those who wish to speak about the candidate. First I'll take those wishing to speak against.' Then, when nobody stirred, 'Those wishing to speak in favour.'

Still nobody stirred, so Shakir Baran felt in duty bound, as the only one who knew the candidate, to take the floor.

'The name Mazlum, as you all know, means "innocent", and Mazlum Inal is, as the name suggests, a most inoffensive and modest man. I know him from our military service days. We both did our time in Polatli. He learned English all by himself. He's a quiet and retiring scholar. I don't think he's published much; that's not because he's lazy but because of his excessive modesty. He's been a lecturer at Erzurum University since it opened. He volunteered to go there.'

Cries of 'Splendid!', 'What more can one ask?', 'Very suitable!' and 'Agreed!'

The Dean put it to the vote: 'Those in favour. Those against. Mazlum Inal has been elected to the Chair of Palaeontology by thirty-one votes to fourteen; seven against and seven abstaining. I am adjourning the meeting for a quarter of an hour.'

Ayetullah Bey was still looking for Ihsan. Finally he gave up hope of finding him and limped to the lift. The fact that he was going to have to pay his own fare home seemed to have tired him more than the physical effort.

Sedat Germiyanoghlu, not wanting to stay for the second act of the comedy, collected his coat and went downstairs. In front of the Faculty post office he saw Jevat, the guru of the pro-Junta group, talking to Sakip Özbashar. Jevat was asking, 'What was that half-wit's name again?'

Sakip Özbashar replied, 'I believe it was Mazlum Inal. They said he was a lecturer at Erzurum University.'

'Let's send him a telegram at once. Take this down: "Have secured your election despite overwhelming odds. Am as pleased as you are. Affectionate regards and congratulations on behalf of my group. Signed, Jevat Sakaoghlu."'

Other Titles from
FOREST BOOKS

Special Collection

THE NAKED MACHINE Selected poems of Matthías Johannessen.
Translated from the *Icelandic* by Marshall Brement.
(Forest/Almenna bokáfélagid)
0 948259 44 2 cloth £7.95   0 948259 43 4 paper £5.95   96 pages.
Ilustrated

ON THE CUTTING EDGE Selected poems of Justo Jorge Padrón.
Translated from the *Spanish* by Louis Bourne.
0 948259 42 6 paper £7.95   176 pages

ROOM WITHOUT WALLS Selected poems of Bo Carpelan.
Translated from the *Swedish* by Anne Born.
0 948259 08 6 paper £6.95   144 pages. Illustrated

CALL YOURSELF ALIVE? The love poems of Nina Cassian.
Translated from the *Romanian* by Andrea Deletant and
Brenda Walker. Introduction by Fleur Adcock.
0 948259 38 8 paper £5.95.   96 pages. Illustrated

RUNNING TO THE SHROUDS Six sea stories of Konstantin
Stanyukovich. Translated from the *Russian* by Neil Parsons.
0 948259 06 X paper £5.95   112 pages.

A VANISHING EMPTINESS Selected poems of Willem Roggeman.
Edited by Yann Lovelock. Translated from the *Dutch*.
0 948259 51 5 £7.95   112 pages. Illustrated

PORTRAIT OF THE ARTIST AS AN ABOMINABLE SNOWMAN
Selected poems of Gabriel Rossenstock translated from the *Irish* by
Michael Hartnett. New Poems translated by Jason Sommer.
Dual text with cassette.
0 948259 56 6 paper £7.95   112 pages

LAND AND PEACE Selected poems of Desmond Egan translated *into*
Irish by Michael Hartnett. Gabriel Rossenstock, Douglas Sealey
and Tomas MacSiomoin. Dual text.
0 948259 64 7 paper £7.95   112 pages

THE EYE IN THE MIRROR Selected poems of Takis Varvitsiotis.
Translated from the *Greek* by Kimon Friar. (Forest/Paratiritis)
0 948259 59 0 paper £8.95   160 pages

THE WORLD AS IF Selected poems of Uffe Harder.
Translated from the *Danish* by John F. Deane and Uffe Harder.
0 948259 76 0 paper £4.95   80 pages

THE TWELFTH MAN Selected poems of Iftighar Arif.
Translated from the *Urdu* by Brenda Walker and Iftighar Arif.
Dual text.
0 948259 49 3 paper £6.95   96 pages

SPRINGTIDES Selected poems of Pia Tafdrup.
Translated from the *Danish* by Anne Born.
0 948259 55 8 paper £6.95   96 pages

SNOW AND SUMMERS Selected poems of Solveig von Schoultz.
Translated from *Finland/Swedish* by Anne Born.
Introduction by Bo Carpelan. Arts Council funded.
0 948259 52 3 paper £7.95   128 pages

HEARTWORK Stories of Solveig von Schoultz.
Translated from *Finland/Swedish* by Marlaine Delargy and
Joan Tate. Introduction by Bo Carpelan.
0 948259 50 7 paper £7.95   128 pages

East European Series

FOOTPRINTS OF THE WIND Selected poems of Mateja Matevski.
Translated from the *Macedonian* by Ewald Osers.
Introduction by Robin Skelton. Arts Council funded.
0 948259 41 8 paper £6.95   96 pages. Illustrated

ARIADNE'S THREAD An anthology of contemporary Polish
women poets. Translated from the *Polish* by Susan Bassnett and
Piotr Kuhiwczak.
UNESCO collection of representative works.
0 948259 45 0 paper £6.95   96 pages

POETS OF BULGARIA An anthology of contemporary Bulgarian poets.
Edited by William Meredith. Introduction by Alan Brownjohn.
0 948259 39 6 paper £6.95   112 pages

FIRES OF THE SUNFLOWER Selected poems by Ivan Davidkov.
Translated from the *Bulgarian* by Ewald Osers.
0 948259 48 5 paper £6.95   96 pages. Illustrated

STOLEN FIRE Selected poems by Lyubomir Levchev.
Translated from the *Bulgarian* by Ewald Osers.
Introduction by John Balaban.
UNESCO collection of representative works.
0 948259 04 3 paper £5.95   112 pages. Illustrated

AN ANTHOLOGY OF CONTEMPORARY ROMANIAN POETRY
Translated by Andrea Deletant and Brenda Walker.
0 9509487 4 8 paper £5.00   112 pages.

GATES OF THE MOMENT Selected poems of Ion Stoica.
Translated from the *Romanian* by Brenda Walker and
Andrea Deletant. Dual text with cassette.
0 9509487 0 5 paper £5.00   126 pages
Cassette £3.50 plus VAT

SILENT VOICES An anthology of contemporary Romanian women
poets. Translated by Andrea Deletant and Brenda Walker.
0 948259 03 5 paper £6.95   172 pages.

EXILE ON A PEPPERCORN Selected poems of Mircea Dinescu.
Translated from the *Romanian* by Andrea Deletant and
Brenda Walker.
0 948259 00 0 paper £5.95   96 pages. Illustrated

LET'S TALK ABOUT THE WEATHER Selected poems of Marin Sorescu.
Translated from the *Romanian* by Andrea Deletant and
Brenda Walker.
0 9509487 8 0 papger £5.95   96 pages.

THE THIRST OF THE SALT MOUNTAIN Three plays by Marin Sorescu
(Jonah, The Verger, and the Matrix).
Translated from the *Romanian* by Andrea Deletant and
Brenda Walker.
0 9509487 5 6 paper £6.95   124 pages. Illustrated

VLAD DRACULA THE IMPALER A play by Marin Sorescu.
Translated from the *Romanian* by Dennis Deletant.
0 948259 07 8 paper £6.95   112 pages. Illustrated

THE ROAD TO FREEDOM Poems and Prose Poems by Geo Milev.
Translated from the *Bulgarian* by Ewald Osers.
UNESCO collection of representative works.
0 948259 40 X paper £6.95   96 pages

IN CELEBRATION OF MIHAI EMINESCU Selected poems and extracts
translated from the *Romanian* by Brenda Walker and
Horia Florian Popescu. Illustrated by Sabin Balaşa.
0 948259 62 0 cloth £14.95   0 948259 63 9 paper £10.95   224 pages

THROUGH THE NEEDLE'S EYE Selected poems of Ion Miloş.
Translated from the *Romanian* by Brenda Walker and Ion Miloş.
0 948259 61 2 paper £6.95   96 pages. Illustrated

YOUTH WITHOUT YOUTH and other Novellas by Mircea Eliade.
Edited and with an introduction by Matei Calinescu.
Translated from the *Romanian* by MacLinscott Ricketts.
0 948259 74 4 paper £12.95   328 pages

A WOMAN'S HEART Stories by Jordan Yovkov.
Translated from the *Bulgarian* by John Burnip.
0 948259 54 X paper £9.95   208 pages

Fun Series

JOUSTS OF APHRODITE Poems collected from the Greek
Anthology Book V.
Translated from the *Greek* into modern English by Michael Kelly.
0 948259 05 1 cloth £6.95   0 94825 34 5 paper £4.95
96 pages